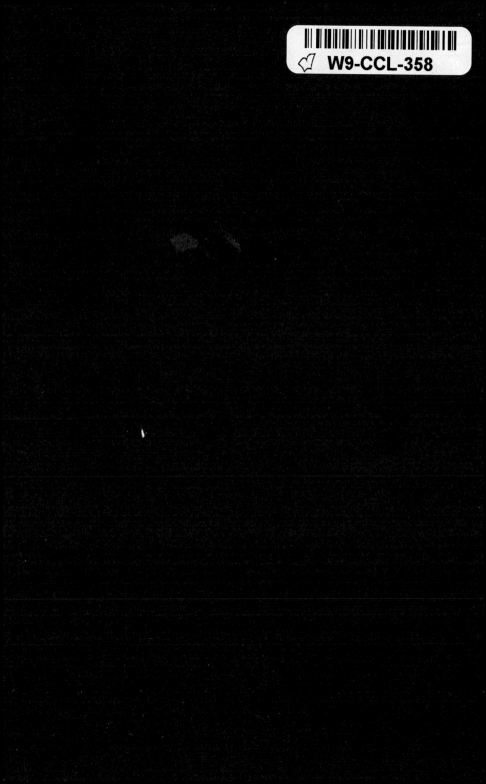

# THE
# SUNDOWN SPEECH

# Books by Loren D. Estleman

## AMOS WALKER MYSTERIES
*Motor City Blue*
*Angel Eyes*
*The Midnight Man*
*The Glass Highway*
*Sugartown*
*Every Brilliant Eye*
*Lady Yesterday*
*Downriver*
*Silent Thunder*
*Sweet Women Lie*
*Never Street*
*The Witchfinder*
*The Hours of the Virgin*
*A Smile on the Face of the Tiger*
*Sinister Heights*
*Poison Blonde**
*Retro**
*Nicotine Kiss**
*American Detective**
*The Left-Handed Dollar**
*Infernal Angels**
*Burning Midnight**
*Don't Look for Me**
*You Know Who Killed Me**
*The Sundown Speech**

## VALENTINO, FILM DETECTIVE
*Frames**
*Alone**
*Alive!**

## DETROIT CRIME
*Whiskey River*
*Motown*
*King of the Corner*
*Edsel*
*Stress*
*Jitterbug**
*Thunder City**

## PETER MACKLIN
*Kill Zone*
*Roses Are Dead*
*Any Man's Death*
*Something Borrowed, Something Black**
*Little Black Dress**

## OTHER FICTION
*The Oklahoma Punk*
*Sherlock Holmes vs. Dracula*
*Dr. Jekyll and Mr. Holmes*
*Peeper*
*Gas City**
*Journey of the Dead**
*The Rocky Mountain Moving Picture Association**
*Roy & Lillie: A Love Story**
*The Confessions of Al Capone**

## PAGE MURDOCK SERIES
*The High Rocks**
*Stamping Ground**
*Murdock's Law**
*The Stranglers*
*City of Widows**
*White Desert**
*Port Hazard**
*The Book of Murdock**

## WESTERNS
*The Hider*
*Aces & Eights**
*The Wolfer*
*Mister St. John*
*This Old Bill*
*Gun Man*
*Bloody Season*
*Sudden Country*
*Billy Gashade**
*The Master Executioner**
*Black Powder, White Smoke**
*The Undertaker's Wife**
*The Adventures of Johnny Vermillion**
*The Branch and the Scaffold**
*Ragtime Cowboys**
*The Long High Noon**

## NONFICTION
*The Wister Trace*
*Writing the Popular Novel*

*Published by Tom Doherty Associates

# THE
# SUNDOWN SPEECH

## An Amos Walker Novel

Loren D. Estleman

A Tom Doherty Associates Book
New York

THE SUNDOWN SPEECH

Copyright © 2015 by Loren D. Estleman

A Forge Book
Published by Tom Doherty Associates, LLC
175 Fifth Avenue
New York, NY 10010

www.tor-forge.com

Forge® is a registered trademark of Tom Doherty Associates, LLC.

Library of Congress Cataloging-in-Publication Data

Estleman, Loren D., author.
    The sundown speech : an Amos Walker novel / by
Loren D. Estleman.—First Edition.
        p. cm.—(Amos Walker novels ; 24)
    ISBN 978-0-7653-3736-8 (hardcover)
    ISBN 978-1-4668-3435-4 (e-book)
    1. Walker, Amos (Fictitious character)—Fiction.    2. Murder—
Investigation—Fiction.    I. Title.
    PS3555.S84S93 2015
    813'.54—dc23

                                                    2015023332

Our books may be purchased in bulk for promotional, educational, or business use. Please contact your local bookseller or the Macmillan Corporate and Premium Sales Department at (800) 221-7945, extension 5442, or by e-mail at MacmillanSpecialMarkets@macmillan.com.

First Edition: November 2015

Printed in the United States of America

0  9  8  7  6  5  4  3  2  1

In memory of Lois Randall, the queen of copy editors
and the best friend I never met

Detroit is working class and sometimes speaks with a foreign accent. It sends its sons and daughters to Ann Arbor to get educated, to get the class that it doesn't have. Ann Arbor is petite and learned, but it happens.

—*Detroit: A Young Guide to the City*

Ann Arbor was at the extreme west end of the habitable world, beyond which the sun went down into a boundless, bottomless morass, where the frightful sound of yelling Indians, howling wolves, croaking frogs, rattling massaugers [sic], and buzzing mosquitoes added to the awful horror of the dismal place.

—Henry Hill, a pioneer of the 1830s

# PART ONE

# SMASH CUT

# ONE

Roll the clock back a dozen years, maybe more; Michael Jackson was still alive, Iris, too. I could walk all day without limping. Tweet was bird talk, the chain bookstore was the greatest threat to civilization since ragtime music, and the only time you saw a black president was in a sci-fi film. Going back is always a crapshoot.

Downtown Ann Arbor was draining into Zingerman's Deli at 11:00 A.M. A chirpy Bohemian girl with her cranberry-colored hair wrapped in a bandanna snood fashion worked her way down the hungry line, taking orders and offering cubes of cheese and curls of lunchmeat impaled on toothpicks, and feet ground away at the black-and-white tiles in dirty sneakers, glossy Florsheims, cork sandals, and nothing at all. In the town that invented the five-dollar fine for possession of marijuana, "no shirt, no shoes, no service" was just a quaint suggestion. In those days you could even smoke tobacco if you didn't mind being glared at.

I'm used to it. I paid for my order and took my receipt outside, to a picnic table to light a cigarette and wait. It was a bright warm day and there were plenty of halter tops and navel piercings to admire.

In a little while an employee carrying a tray with a side of pork pressed between thick slabs of sourdough asked me politely to put out the butt. I did that. My clients had arrived, anyway. I got up to meet them.

They fit the description I'd gotten over the telephone, the woman straight-haired and graying, no makeup, wearing a dress of some unbleached material that hung from straps on her shoulders like a sandwich board, the man trailing a couple of steps behind in corduroys and a soft shirt with the collar spread, gray at the temples, with the pinched expression of an actor in an aspirin commercial. They wore identical glasses with no rims.

The indigenous local species: *Homo Arboritis.*

"Amos Walker? My goodness, you *look* like a detective. I'm Heloise Gunnar. This is Dante."

No other identification, i.e. *Dante, my husband.* It was no business of mine.

Her grip was firm, the hand corded with muscle. His hand fluttered in mine and was gone. I let the detective crack go and we sat facing each other on opposite benches.

"What do you think of Zingerman's?" Heloise Gunnar said. "We thought as long as you were coming out from the city, you might as well sample a native institution. It's always being written up in travel magazines."

"I thought maybe you picked it because it's on Detroit Street. Make me feel at home." The place looked as far away from the Motor City as Morocco. You only saw open-air crowds like that in the Farmers Market, where there's strength in numbers.

"Is it? We're hardly aware of street names anymore. Dante was born right here in town, and I came out after I graduated Berkeley."

"That would be in the sixties?"

The skin whitened a shade around her nostrils. She had some vanity after all under the patchouli. "Seventy-four. I majored in English Lit. I don't get to use as much of it as you'd think managing a bookstore."

After football and stoplights, Ann Arbor majors in bookstores. Managing one is no more a topic of dinner conversation there than pouring steel in Gary.

"What do you do, Mr.—?" I asked. So far he hadn't said a word.

"Gunnar." He lifted his brows. "Didn't you hear my wife?"

So they were married; or as good as. I said something about not every wife taking her husband's surname.

"I work for the U of M." He made it sound as if there was no alternative other than shelving books. "Information Services."

That meant exactly nothing to me. I'd only asked out of politeness. It was that stage of the relationship.

Our meals came, borne by a left tackle with a block M tattooed on one forearm. I had rare roast beef and cheddar on an onion roll, Heloise Gunnar portabello mushrooms on whole wheat, Dante something that looked like sphagnum moss between coarse slices of unleavened bread. His eyes followed my red meat like a dog's. There's no reason for all this detail other than I've made a habit of it. You can tell a lot about a client from what he eats, and even more from what he doesn't.

We made dents in the bill of fare and washed everything down with our drinks of choice. I had black coffee, the Gunnars mineral water with no fizz. I wondered if they flew this close to type when they weren't in public.

"You were recommended to us by Dr. Albierti." Heloise dabbed at the corners of her wide unpainted mouth with a brown paper napkin. "He's a professor emeritus with thirty years in Romance Languages. You freed his daughter from a cult."

"She joined the Young Republicans," I said. "I found her living in Saline with a professional lobbyist. I told her to call home; that was the job. Did she?"

"Yes. He sent her money. She's married to a yoga instructor here in town. So we know you get results. Missing persons, that's your specialty, right?"

The roast beef was fidgeting uneasily in my stomach. I'd begun to suspect a practical joke. It had Barry Stackpole all over it. If she said she was Wiccan I was going to pull the plug on the interview.

"Who's missing?"

"Jerry Marcus." A bit of moss clung to Dante's lower lip. He flinched when Heloise reached out and swept it away with her napkin.

"Jerry Marcus," she said, as if he hadn't spoken. "He's an *auteur*. Do you know the term?"

"It's a film director who reads subtitles. Does anyone in your circle operate a forklift?"

"I don't know what that is. Jerry's an independent. One of the new breed: digital. He does most of it on a computer. We met him at a party in the Michigan Union, where he was raising money for his first commercial project. Do you know much about science fiction, Mr. Walker?"

"I get a lot of it from clients. But you tell it, Mrs. Gunnar. You're covering the meal."

"Dante and I prefer *Ms.* I almost didn't take his name, you were right about that. It was never a legal requirement. But when you're born Gilhooley, you make certain concessions. Jerry's script, which he wrote himself, is about aliens from a planet run by a totalitarian regime come to earth to clone both front-runners for the office of President of the United States. He's filming every last foot here in town and in the suburbs. He brought along a disc of what he'd shot and showed it to us on his laptop. He's made a very effective use of the smash cut. Do you know what that is?"

I said I didn't; I had to throw her one. She got animated then; up to that point she'd been Wednesday Addams.

"A smash cut is a quick camera transition to a new scene, punctuated by a sudden loud noise, designed to shock the audience. You know, like when a quiet scene is pierced by a phone ringing shrilly. The sound effect belongs to the next scene, but you hear it while the first is still on screen. It wakes people up."

"Maybe if the quiet scene was cut, they wouldn't fall asleep. How much did you invest?"

"How did you—? Oh, yes, I suppose it's obvious. Fifteen thousand; fifty percent of the budget, with millions to be made if the film opens. *Opens,* that's what they say when it's a success right off the bat. These days, if it isn't, it's as if it was never released in the first place. *The Blair Witch Project,* that opened and how. It was shot on a shoestring and outstripped everything the studios pumped millions into that year, including *Fight Club,* starring Brad Pitt. We made the check out on the spot and signed a contract that required him to provide an accounting in six months. That was nine months ago."

"He took a powder."

She glanced down at the front of her dress, looking for powder. "Disappeared," I said. "You should watch a movie sometime without a little green man in it. Did you try to get in touch with him?"

She glared at me through her glasses. The lenses were thick; it was like looking at two angry planets through an electron telescope. She hadn't liked that last crack.

"If we hadn't, would we be meeting with you?"

"I can probably find him, if he isn't in a landfill. I can almost guarantee that when I do it won't include the fifteen grand. Not all of it anyway."

"Any portion would be welcome. At the very least, if he's absconded with our money, we'll have the satisfaction of seeing him prosecuted. Do you carry a firearm, Mr. Walker?"

"The governor says I can. Do you think it's that kind of a job?"

"Definitely not. Dante and I are major contributors to

the gun control lobby in Washington. You must promise us that your gun will remain locked up at home, or wherever you keep it, throughout the investigation. We can't have someone's death on our conscience."

"No dice. Call Greenpeace."

"In that case, this interview is over. What do we owe you for the consultation?" She jerked open a handbag made of burlap fastened with a drawstring.

"Damn it, Hel!"

She jumped. I almost did. I'd had Dante down for some throat operation that prevented him from raising his voice above a murmur. He'd taken another nervous bite of his sandwich, and the spot of green against the color of his face looked like Christmas.

"Do you know how many press releases I have to write in order to make fifteen thousand dollars? It isn't as if you make commissions on those books you sell. You could do better in tips working in this restaurant."

If his wife's eyes were suns instead of planets they'd set him on fire through those heavy-duty lenses. But she said nothing.

That clinched it for me. "I get five hundred a day," I said. "Three days in advance, to cover the cost of ammo."

I'd tossed that in to see if she'd balk. She didn't, although when her gaze shifted to mine I almost ducked back into the anthill. I finished my sandwich while she made out the check. They really know how to make beef sing at Zingerman's.

# TWO

The check was on dirty-looking recycled paper with an engraved sketch of something that suggested a cross between a manatee and Meatloaf, undoubtedly an endangered species. Heloise Gunnar gave it to me along with some start-up information and a clipping from the *Ann Arbor News* about Jerry Marcus' moviemaking project. In the photo, a thirtyish elfin face beamed out from under a mop of curly dark hair, with a chin suitable for driving flathead screws. He looked like a chiseler, but then the really successful ones never do.

"The paper might have another contact number," I said. "Did you ask?"

She shook her head. "They endorsed the conservative ticket in the last election. We canceled our subscription the next day."

"I'll start there. The last time I voted, the candidates' wives all wore girdles."

"That would be LBJ?" Her smile was shrink-sealed to

her face. Here was a woman who could carry a grudge to the grave.

"Wilson. I marched with the Bonus Army. I don't guess you tried the police."

"Those fascists?"

I said I'd call, and saw them out to their car. It was a faded-rose Volvo—the closest thing to a Birkenstock on wheels—plastered all over the rear panel with peace signs and slogans. It probably ran on soybeans.

My Cutlass was parked at a one-hour meter around the corner. I put the overtime ticket in the glove compartment with the others and checked the load in the Chief's Special I keep in a spring hatch under the dash. I went weeks without doing that or even thinking about it, but Heloise's convictions had made me superstitious on top of my indigestion. I figured they poured the hot sauce with welders' gloves and a pair of tongs.

I hadn't caved in yet to carrying a cell; you could still find a public telephone then without a historic plaque in front of it. I found one and tried the number Marcus had given the Gunnars, confirmed it was out of service, and called the number I got for the *News* from the directory chained to the box.

"What is it you want, Mr. Walker?" asked a cool female voice belonging to the features editor.

"Information. Isn't that your business?"

"A newspaper's business is to make money. We provide the material that attracts readers to our advertisers, based on circulation figures. At least, that's what the people who draw up our ads say," she said with a sigh.

"Give me something they can get their teeth into, and we'll talk."

"A local moviemaker's gone missing," I said. "It could be a flimflam, or foul play. Things may have changed, but when I grew up, those things sold papers."

"Is this about Jerry Marcus?" If you can feel a thermometer jump a couple of degrees, I felt it at that moment.

I said it was, and told her his cell was out of service.

"We might have another number. Are you free this afternoon?"

The *News* building was a cream-colored Deco pile on Huron Street, a couple of blocks off Main. I rode a rheumatic elevator up to the press room, sandwiched between a stuttering fluorescent ceiling and a linoleum floor that had sunk so far into the boards beneath it made me seasick just walking down the aisle. The chunky typewriters of legend had given way to pre-Columbian computer consoles mounted on desks made of pressed cardboard. The first time I'd visited a newspaper office, on East Lafayette, the clatter of Underwood manuals and rumble of cylinder presses in the basement underfoot was like a shot of adrenaline; in this digital age, the keyboards sounded like an old lady coughing discreetly into a handkerchief.

The place smelled of rubber cement and toner, which was the formula for the coffee I drank with the editor, a pleasant-faced woman with the eyes of a peregrine falcon. We sat facing each other across a desk of no particular design in an office separated from the rest of the floor by pebbled-glass partitions that didn't reach to the ceiling. Plaques and framed certificates added to the general clutter of paper and personal memorabilia; a cube on the desk kept changing family pictures, a distraction I tried hard to ignore.

"I know," she said, when I reacted to the coffee. "We make it with bottled water: all the good minerals filtered out, at three times the cost of the spring water they started with. They strain it and distill it and refine it until nothing's left. Just like the newspaper business."

"What's wrong with it? The newspaper business."

"Oh, it's okay. Where I spent my internship, the rewrite man was a character out of MacArthur and Hecht. He had a telephone line installed in the corner booth of the bar across the street from the paper, and he worked there from opening to last call. Never went to the office. A reporter on the scene of a fire would call him, spew out the details, and he'd rap out something in five minutes that sounded like Hemingway. He was a drunk and a bigot, but what he wrote had balls. You don't get quite the same thing on mocha latte."

"Finished?" I said.

She flushed. She was in a landing pattern around middle age, with dyed-beige hair and a stroke of blush on each cheek. I'd have taken her for a benevolent aunt but for those eyes. They were like steel shavings.

"Finished. If I didn't do this once a month, I'd wind up on the Washington Press Corps, taking dictation from the president. I've had offers."

"I'm sure you have. Do you know about Jerry Marcus?"

The eyes glazed over. "What was your name again?"

I told her again. Journalists, like lawyers, are hell for repetition. This time she scribbled in the reporters' pad at her elbow; the first time seemed to have been practice. She'd missed it the same way Rosa Parks missed the bus.

"My clients gave this fellow Marcus money to shoot his picture," I said, "then fell out of touch. There might be nothing in it."

She looked at my ID, screwed up her forehead at the deputy's star pinned to the bottom of the folder.

I shrugged. "Bureaucratic oversight. The county forgot to ask for it back after I gave up serving papers."

"Isn't it illegal to carry it?"

"It is."

"Are you always this honest?"

"No. But I could be lying."

"Any personal references?"

I gave her some names and numbers and rolled the Styrofoam cup between my palms while she made the calls. A faux-knitted sampler in a folksy barkwood frame hung at an angle behind her head, reading: DON'T PAINT THE DEVIL AS BLACK AS HE IS. Everything means something to somebody.

She spent three minutes apiece on each call. She made some squiggles in a notepad, then hung up. A nerve twitched in her right cheek. "You're not a popular person, are you?"

"I kind of languished when teams were picked," I said. "I played dirty."

"Not when it counted, I was most reluctantly told."

"The people who like me wouldn't impress you."

"I wrote that article myself," she said. "It's a pretty big deal when someone makes a movie here. The climate, you know; those smogtown crews are terrified of going over schedule and seeing what their breath looks like in late

November. Even when the picture's set in Ann Arbor, they shoot it in L.A., with about three days' worth of second-unit footage here for the exteriors. What's one definition of a Michigan native?"

"Someone who's never met a celebrity."

"So when snow falls in Death Valley and a legitimate outfit shoots locally, we put it on the front page. We get a bump in circulation and maybe sell an ad or two when the movie premieres." She frowned. "A lot of folks are going to be disappointed if Marcus turns out to be just another swindler. That's a daily item around here."

"It's what I'm being paid to find out."

"Do we get the story?"

"If it's fraud, you'll get it before the cops. If it's something more serious, I've got a license to stand in front of."

"In that event, I'll have to give it to the city desk. The newspaper business is run on a feudal system, and God help the reporter who turns in the murder of a football player to anyone but the sports editor."

Her Rolodex rattled like a bingo basket. When it stopped, she scribbled something on the back of a business card she took from her desk and gave it to me. The telephone number was local.

"It's a landline," she said. "Campus area, I think. Marcus gave it to me when I interviewed him."

I stuck it in my wallet. "I appreciate the time. I know how busy you get this time of day."

Her face softened. She was an attractive woman when she let herself be. "First time in town?"

"I come through now and then, never long enough to soak

up the atmosphere. Mostly I work Detroit, the northern suburbs, and Downriver. Any dragons I need to know about?"

"East side's dicey, and you want to watch yourself in the
nightclubs; but where you're going, burglary's as bad as it
usually gets. Couch fires were a problem until the city
banned upholstered furniture on porches. Some were ar-
son, others caused by kids learning how to smoke. It's a
nice town, once you get past the attitude."

"What attitude's that?"

"Oh, it's an old saw."

"I'm old enough to appreciate it."

She had one of those tri-cornered rules on her desk; the
kind old-time schoolteachers used to rap the alphabet
across errant knuckles. She picked it up and slid it between
the thumb and forefinger of one hand; dragging something
up from some depth.

"A long time ago," she said, "someone told them Ann
Arbor's the cultural center of the world, and they haven't
gotten the joke yet."

"*They* being who?"

She gave me an edited smile. "If your clients are who I
think they are, you've met two of them."

"I didn't know the place was that small."

"Not as small as some of the residents like to pretend.
The population runs around a hundred thousand when
university's in session. But this is the only daily, not counting the student rag, and it isn't my first. Here you can get
hold of a copy of *Beowulf* translated into Frangi, which is
a language that only existed for three weeks in the eleventh
century, but you can't buy a decent cup of coffee anywhere

in town." She sipped from her mug, blue with a yellow block M printed on it, and grimaced.

"I must have passed half a dozen coffee shops on the way here from the deli."

"A new one opens every month or so and lasts about as long as Frangi. When I came here, you could still buy nails by the pound in hardware stores downtown. Now you have to go out to the big-box joints by the malls. In twenty years the place will be wall-to-wall cafes and brew pubs. And the university, of course, gobbling up millions in donations and tax-free real estate."

"You make it sound like you were here when they poured the first sidewalk."

"Not so long, really. The place keeps making itself over. The only thing that never changes is the attitude."

I grinned. "Frangi, seriously? Does everyone in town have a Ph.D.?"

She colored a little. "The place drips with erudition. Don't get me wrong; I love it here. The people are friendly, by and large, the bookstores are great, and you can walk through downtown after midnight any day of the week, safe in a crowd. But sometimes you want to go to a place where people double their negatives and think Fellini's something you can order at Olive Garden."

I emptied my cup, just to prove what a tough character I am, and got up.

"Thanks for the number. Also the lowdown."

She smiled. "Got your first parking ticket yet?"

"They nailed me outside Zingerman's."

"You get used to it."

# THREE

I found another public phone; that's how good a detective I am. Even the homeless party camped on the sidewalk among his overstuffed trash bags had his broker on his cell.

No answer at the new number. When the cheerful recorded voice of Ma Bell cut in telling me to try again later, I waggled the plunger and dialed a number I knew by heart.

"Where are you?" Barry Stackpole asked, when I identified myself. "You sound like you're calling from the hull of an oil tanker."

"Pay phone in Ann Arbor."

"No shit. Museum of Natural History?"

"There are a couple of dodos left."

"Going back for your master's?"

"I've got a number that won't answer. I need an address to go with it."

"Anything for me?"

"You're the second reporter who's asked me that today. Don't you people ever take a break?"

"Waiting for an answer."

"I already promised dibs. You're next, unless there's bleeding involved."

"You're in luck. I'm online right now, exploring the mysteries of the Vatican."

"The pope's mobbed up?"

"Can't say, but there's a cardinal who finds it way too easy to get World Cup tickets. Give me a sec. I uploaded all the reverse directories in the metropolitan area just last month."

"Aren't those fire department property?"

"What's your point?" Keys clattered on his end.

Barry was living on the west side of Detroit that year, in a HUD home-turned-crackhouse-turned-abandoned-shell he'd bought from the city for the sum of one dollar and the promise to rescue it from urban blight. He'd sunk most of his 401(k) from his time as an investigative reporter for the *Detroit News* into replacing the wiring and plumbing, scavenged by the local scrap rats, a new roof, and exterminators; every time one of those vans pulls into a driveway, the rats and roaches boil out in all directions like dust from a controlled demolition. His settling in was a good sign; since a mob pineapple had blown off one leg, two fingers, and part of his skull, he'd been in the habit of changing addresses as often as the Ten Most Wanted.

"Yahtzee," he said. "It's a residential address on Thompson Street." He gave me the number.

"Thanks, buddy. If it turns out to be nothing, there's a bottle of Scotch with your name on it."

"Fuck my name. It better start with Glen."

The house was off State Street, the main drag running through the University of Michigan campus. Thompson was mostly student housing, around the corner from Borders books; not the store Heloise Gunnar managed. It's still student housing, but Borders is long gone, a victim of over-ambition and bad choices regarding the Internet. Back then it was jumping, with browsers wandering the aisles beyond plate glass and checking out the bargains on tables outside. It was the flagship of the fleet, the first big-box bookshop, founded by two brothers under Richard Nixon. I think it's a coffee shop now.

I waited through a couple of light changes. The system was operated by a thirty-year-old computer, and when green finally came up, the first driver in line always went through the same four-step process: 1. realization; 2. comprehension; 3. mechanical analysis; 4. acceleration. Only in Ann Arbor, and every time I visited.

Jaywalking 101 had just let out as I approached campus. I tooted my horn and got a choreograph of raised middle fingers in response. When a space opened up I turned the corner and parked in a parallel slot a block from my destination. Yellow parking tickets decorated most of the windshields on the block. I fed the meter tight.

The house was a two-story frame with tile siding, yellowed to the standard shade of bad dental hygiene. A sagging front porch supported a dirty red-velour sofa and two young people drinking from red plastic Solo cups.

One wore his hair in cornrows, the other mowed his close to the scalp. Both wore Michigan basketball jerseys, baggy cargo shorts, and cross-trainers with the laces dangling. I asked the one seated closest to me if Jerry Marcus lived there. A full set of studs turned my way. It was female.

"Sorry, mister. Grandpa's already cast."

"I'm investing, not auditioning." I held up a dollar bill.

An arm with barbed wire circling it in blue ink swept out and fisted the bill. "Upstairs, all the way back."

"Thanks. I thought couches on porches were illegal in this town."

"Also underage drinking." She drank from her cup and belched beer. Cornrows snorted a giggle and dragged half a Marlboro deep into his lungs.

The screen door grated against the pressure of its spring and slapped shut behind me. It opened directly into a small dim living room with mismatched furniture and an orange shag carpet that had been shampooed the week Saigon fell. Something moved sluggishly in an aquarium on a stand, glistening emerald green in the light from the window next to it. I wondered if there was a local length limit on pet boa constrictors.

The stairs were bare and the banister wobbled. I left it alone and ascended freeform. The smell of fries cooked in day-old grease increased in direct ratio to the distance I put between myself and the kitchen on the ground floor. I wondered if they still made hot plates or if the tenants had built their own fires from the wooden rods missing from the banister.

Mice had chewed abstract patterns in the rubber runner

in the upstairs hallway. The window at the end was painted over. There were ceiling canisters with bulbs in them, but nothing happened when I flipped a switch on the wall. I groped my way down the tunnel, past a bathroom with its door open and fish swimming on a plastic shower curtain. On the evidence the toilet brush had been burned along with the stair rods.

It was typical student housing. Dostoevsky would have recognized it from Minsk City College.

Near the end I tested the invisible wall for breaks. When I ran out of plaster I brushed a wooden panel with a knuckle. The door squeaked open. I stepped inside, rapping on the frame to announce myself. No one called out. No footsteps came.

"Aw, hell."

I jumped at the sound of the voice, even though it was mine. I felt like I hadn't spoken in days. It was just premonition; but I always test well above average on that subject.

It was just the one room. He'd have to share the bathroom outside with his neighbors. A chipped ceramic skillet on a Coleman stove turned a rolling TV cart into a kitchen. Clothes and books scattered the carpet, green and rubbery and discolored from sun and stain. The fibers crunched underfoot. What I thought at first to be someone sleeping turned out to be a twisted heap of bedding on a twin mattress. Brass paint curled off the iron frame in paper-thin scraps. A poster of *Das Boot* clung to the wall above the bed, stuck to it with curls of tape leaving telltale bulges at the corners. The U-boat seemed to be streaming straight toward me, torpedo tubes wide open.

A white CRT computer monitor glowed with a sullen hum on a student desk. The screensaver was a shifting montage of black-and-white images: Welles in *Citizen Kane,* Mastroanni in *La Dolce Vita,* Stallone in *Rocky,* others I didn't recognize. Those I did were all the work of independent filmmakers. No surprises so far. The place could have been done by a set decorator with a clear understanding of the kind of character who would live there.

Some no-shows stuck out: film cans, reels, a projector, all absent. I'd always thought *auteurs* slept with their equipment. A sleek ruby-red camera, probably digital, lay on the floor beside the bed. It was about the size of a deck of cards but less than half as thick. It seemed a careless way to treat an expensive item like that; but artists are supposed to be eccentric. I'd heard.

The room smelled a lot worse than eccentric, as if no one had taken out the garbage in days.

I broke another law and frisked the place. Sweatshirts, jeans, socks, and underwear in a cheap slap-together dresser, a pair of horn-rim glasses in the nonmatching nightstand. I picked them up without unfolding the bows and peered through the lenses. Window glass: a prop, maybe. I put them back. Someone had built shelves by laying planks across stacks of bricks and filled them with spavined books: *Hitchcock/Truffaut, The Coen Brothers, Eisenstein, The Three Stooges.*

That last one had to be a clue. I slipped it out, riffled through the pages, held it upside down by the covers and shook it. A Borders bookmark fluttered to the floor. I picked it up. Nothing written on either side but advertising.

Sometimes a cigar is just a cigar.

I slipped it back into its place and stood in the middle of the room with my fists on my hips, looking around. Everything else had probably been there when he moved in. No caller ID on the cordless telephone, but I punched redial. The little screen on the handset gave me an exchange and number I didn't recognize. I hung up before anyone answered; I had to know a lot more before I spoke to whoever it was. I wrote the number in my notebook.

I let the computer alone. I don't know anything about them.

I realized I was breathing through my mouth. The room seemed to stink worse than when I'd entered. I felt the same drop in temperature I'd felt then.

There was one more place to look.

It was a narrow door hinged to a compartment built into the wall to hold an ironing board. I pulled it open and stepped back, but no board swung out. Neither did Jerry Marcus. He was stuffed in too tight for that, and stiff as the blood in his curly hair. The bullet hadn't done anything for his boyish good looks.

# FOUR

looked at the watch on his right wrist. It was intact: No smashed face, no time of death. I didn't search the body. There were people who got paid to do that sort of handling.

I spent the time looking the room over with new eyes. The carpet had stood more abuse than one tenant could provide; I detected several generations of cats, and a string of keggers reaching back to the old Stroh's plant.

Other stains were more recent. Splinters of what looked like fine china clung to a dark elliptical blotch the size of a dessert dish. I'd seen that circular fragment pattern before. It said someone had forced Marcus into a prone position, probably on his stomach, and shot him execution style at close range; the fragments were pieces of skull. But there were people who were paid to spend more time on that too. I was satisfied he'd been killed in the room and his body jammed into the cupboard to slow down discovery.

Other items in the mess were harder to explain. What at

first appeared to be more bits of skull turned out to be soft and springy when I picked one up and pressed it between thumb and forefinger. Styrofoam. It looked as if someone with nervous fingers had shredded his coffee cup during intense conversation. The problem with that was it could have happened at any time and had nothing to do with murder. I shook the piece loose and let it fall.

That was it for the crime scene. Others with the right tools could sift through what I hadn't the training or patience for, and the sooner the better.

Clues, phooey. A shred of tobacco, a candy wrapper, a footprint in the dust, bits of red clay unique to El Valle de los Dios in Quetzaltenango, a moustache follicle, a drop of sweat from Custer's left nut, preserved in a plastic case like an Indian-head penny; they're all significant, or all irrelevant, or some combination of both; close your eyes and stab a finger and follow it up. When Inspector Finch-Hatton is on the case, a half-eaten peanut-butter-and-jelly sandwich can crack it wide open. Settle for a sleuth named Walker, and it's just somebody's leftovers.

Most often it's a break in an established pattern of behavior, a slip of the tongue in conversation, a shadow in the wrong place in a picture taken at a certain time on a certain day; something as intangible as a memory you might only have dreamt, and that slips away as easily. An analyst's couch is a more useful tool in the work than a dustpan and a magnifying glass.

I hovered over the cordless phone, then lifted the receiver and pecked out 911. My prints were already on it and the cops could yell at me only so loud.

The operator repeated the word "murder" as if she were taking an order for lunch. They're all the same, even in a town where the occasional break-in was page one news; all the emotion of a white-noise machine running on a low battery.

After I hung up I went back downstairs and out to the porch. The bald girl was in the same position, balancing the plastic cup on a leg enveloped in green canvas with pleated pockets. The boy in cornrows snored on the other end of the sofa with his head jammed into a corner. I envied him his flexible youth. When he woke up he probably wouldn't even have a stiff neck.

I sat between them. A seceding spring poked me in the haunch. The girl saw me wince.

"That's why we don't sit in the middle." She was watching me now with a spark of interest: One buck can always lead to another.

I shifted my weight away from the prod and crossed my legs. "When's the last time you saw Marcus?"

"He wasn't there? You spent a long time up there."

"I waited. When was the last time?"

"You still investing?"

"No. Bottom fell out of the market. When?"

She lowered her eyelids. A bit of metal glinted in one. It set my teeth on edge. "You're like a cop?"

"I'm like a cop." I didn't ask again. I couldn't shorten it any more except to a grunt.

"Ask Sean. He lives here. I just hang."

"That Sean?" I tilted my head toward the snoring boy.

"Uh-huh."

"I can't wait for spring. I'm still asking you."

"Must've been game day," she said.

"Game day?"

"Football! Jeez. Where you from?"

I waited.

"Saturday. When the game's in town we hang and watch the jock-lovers honk at each other trying to get to the Big House and back. It's better than Animal Planet." Her nose ring jiggled when she snorted. "It's so bogus. Bunch of meatheads piling up on each other over what? A dead pig."

"What time?"

"It was about dark; traffic was thinning out. Jerry came out of the house carrying a box."

"What kind of box?"

"A box! Jeez. Cardboard. Square. You know, a box. Had a picture of something on the side, a toaster oven or something. I remember, 'cause I asked him what was in it, like I cared. Only it didn't seem polite not to say anything. I guess he didn't hear me, though. He put the box in his car and got in and drove off. I'm pretty sure that's the last time I saw him."

"What was he driving?"

"Old Mustang convertible, yellow. Viagra-mobile, you know?"

"How well you know Marcus?"

"Not. When I heard he made movies I asked was he looking for actresses. He said no. That was our longest conversation."

"You an actress?"

"When I'm with Sean."

The police came to rescue me from that exchange. They pulled up without flashers or siren, in a city cruiser driven by a uniform with a man in plainclothes on the passenger side. I hauled myself up from the sofa.

"Are you Mr. Walker?"

Plainclothes was built like a peasant farmer. His hair started almost at the bridge of his nose and grew black and shiny as licorice to his collar. They couldn't tailor a suit that would fit him looser than the membrane on a peach. He shook my hand and read my credentials, which I'd taken out of the badge folder. Most of the Detroit cops I deal with know me, but he might be a stickler.

"I'm Lieutenant Karyl." He showed me his ID. A Hungarian name from the spelling.

He asked me some questions he seemed to know the answers to already, left his driver with Sean and his friend, and followed me upstairs with a palm on my back, as if I might bolt. Even climbing single file there was barely space for his shoulders.

Inside Marcus' room he wrinkled his nose at the stench, *tsk-tsked* at the corpse folded and packed like a shirt, squatted over the new stain on the carpet, picked up one of the Styrofoam fragments, sniffed at it, and scraped if off his fingers into a Ziploc bag along with some others he'd scooped off the floor. He put the bag back in his pocket and stood. His pale blue eyes went as deep as the brass plating on the bed.

"What phone did you use to call?"

"That one."

He *tsk-tsked* again. "No cell?"

"Why does everybody ask me that?"

"We'll need your prints."

"State cops have them."

"What's the job?"

"Marcus makes movies. He promised my clients a return on their investment, then lost touch."

"Who are your clients?"

"That's confidential."

"No good."

"It's as good as it gets until I clear it with them."

He reached inside his suit coat, exposing the fisted butt of a Glock in a holster on his belt, and held out a sleek silver phone. "Call them."

I shook my head. "Just because I don't carry one doesn't mean I don't know anything about them. It'd be the same as telling you their number."

"If they think he swindled them, they're good suspects."

"You wouldn't if you met them."

"I'll be asking again." He put his phone away. "Who are your friends outside?"

"Couple of strays." I told them what we'd talked about.

"You said you were a cop?"

"She asked if I was *like* a cop, and I said I was. It's not the same thing."

"I wouldn't want to live on the difference." He looked down at Marcus. "Thank God I haven't had the chance to become an expert, but I'd say this happened not long after the girl saw him last. We'll find out if anyone saw him when he came back."

We returned to the porch. Sean wasn't much more help awake than asleep. He hadn't lived in the house long enough to know anything more about Marcus than his girlfriend did; the frat house he'd lived in before that had shut down when the university yanked its credentials for serving alcohol to minors. The cop in uniform was clearer on the police-impersonation point than the lieutenant, but then the EMS van came and after it the forensics team and Karyl seemed to forget all about it. He gave instructions and then we waited. It was a balmy afternoon in early fall, no nip yet. The leaves hadn't started to turn.

A crowd was gathering on the sidewalk. More police arrived to deal with it, and by the time the body bag came out the barricades were in place. A woman wearing steel-framed glasses and a pantsuit followed it out, carrying a coroner's tackle box.

"What do you think, Doctor?" Karyl asked her.

She walked past him without turning her head. "He's dead. Do I look like the Science Guy?"

He made a dry sound in his throat. "You should see how she gets when somebody calls her Doc."

We retreated upstairs, where the crew in latex were putting away their gizmos. The photographer was checking his results on his little screen; no popped flashbulbs, no Polaroid litter, no chemicals back at the office. I'd been at too many homicide scenes over too many years. I hope to be retired when they give it all to drones.

Karyl told a Hispanic kid going over the cordless phone with a black light that I'd pawed the thing. That bought me a bleak look.

A pretty young Asian woman got up from the floor. A square of carpet had been cut out where the bloodstain had been. She held up a bloody hunk of metal in a glassine bag. "Thirty-eight; maybe three-fifty-seven mag. The scales will tell."

"What about the glasses, prescription?" Karyl asked.

She took another bag out of a pocket and showed him the horn-rims. "Drugstore readers, sorry. Very low magnification. He was only slightly impaired."

I felt older then. I'd thought they were clear glass.

When the print man or whatever they called him told him Marcus' computer was clear, Karyl drew up a chair.

"We know Marcus," he said. "He applied for permits to shoot on public property. If he was scamming your clients, he made it look good. If they'd called us when he went missing, the trail might still be warm."

"They're not fans of the police department."

"Who is, until they need us?" He tapped a key. The movie montage vanished.

"A sergeant I know studies film at the U of M; no one in this town is a cop or a waiter or a pizza guy, they're all writing screenplays. He says the business will all be digital in a few years. Everything shot on disc and edited on a computer."

"How's your screenplay coming along?"

"Not me, Jack. I'm the only cop in the department." He flexed his fingers and hovered above the keys.

"Don't you need a password?"

"Permit clerk's name is Pilsner," he said, as if I hadn't

spoken. "When Marcus kept bending his ear about Bergman, Pilsner told him the Michigan Theater shows *Casa-
blanca* free for students the first week of classes. Marcus
said, 'Wrong Bergman.' The clerk had never heard of Ing-
mar. Maybe I'm not the only working stiff in town after
all." He typed I-N-G-M-A-R. The computer came back
saying the password was incorrect. Same thing when he
tried B-E-R-G-M-A-N.

"Try them both," I said.

He did. A white bar appeared onscreen and began to fill
from left to right. "I'll be damned," he said.

The bar filled quickly. A new screen appeared, stacked
with names of files. Karyl scrolled through them, stopped
at MR. ALIEN ELECT. "If that's not just a working title,
your clients were screwed from day one." He selected it.

A new screen came up. Objects began moving.

It was like watching a TV movie, only the action had a
dream quality, like people running underwater. Marcus'
script called for the extraterrestials to spontaneously
combust to avoid capture; they kept going up like bottle
rockets. It looked cheesy, but maybe on the big screen,
with music and sound effects, it would play like *Lawrence
of Arabia.* You could put everything I know about moviemaking in a shot glass. The locations were all in the neighborhood. I recognized the common area of campus known
as the Diag, with its obsidian cube perched on one of its
corners like a giant die, the bell tower, and some university buildings on State Street. The house we were in appeared, an establishing shot. The camera began to dolly
in. There was no dialogue.

"Whatever this guy did with the fifteen grand, he didn't spend it on cab fare," Karyl said.

Seeing the house reminded me of something.

"What do you think was in that box Marcus carried out to his car Saturday?"

"Toaster oven, probably. Who says a box can't be just a box?"

I barely heard him. "Can you pause?"

He flicked a key. The image froze.

"What do you see?" he asked.

I pointed at a car parked in front of the house on the screen; the house Heloise and Dante didn't know about because they'd lost contact with Jerry Marcus. The color was a little off. The Volvo looked more coppery than pale rose. But all the Gunnars' bumper stickers were in place.

# FIVE

I told him about the Gunnars then; had to. They were suspects now.

"There's no law against lying to a private cop," Karyl said. "But hiring one to find a guy you killed is batty even for a couple of recovered hippies."

"Which is just what they might want you to think."

"That only works in movies, and not for long even then. You'd have to have ice in your veins to stand the risk. Most killers don't, though as I said I'm no authority on that. A psychopath, maybe. What are the odds of two psychopaths getting hitched?"

"Maybe there's a Web site."

A pair of flat blue eyes turned my way. "This funny to you?"

"Relax. It's a defense mechanism." I lit a cigarette. The crime scene posse had cleared out, but the smell of death lingered. "Maybe they got nervous waiting for the body to be found. A thing like that can weigh you down if you're not used to it."

"Who says they're not?"

"Fair question. Maybe they've left a string of dead movie producers leading all the way back to Berkeley. If you saw them you wouldn't be so sure. Ma and Pa Barker they ain't."

"I hope to hell you're right. Dante works for the university, you said. The zillionaire alumni get all worked up when it looks like the local law's beating up on the old Maize and Blue. They threaten to throw it off the tit, the sports program dries up, the university president rags on the mayor, the mayor rags on the chief, and I wind up staring at a bank of monitors on the midnight shift at Holiday Inn. My daughter's a freshman. She'll take it hard if she has to transfer to Washtenaw Community College."

He banged a key, hurling Jerry Marcus' aliens back into space. "I'll talk to them, but only after I talk to the neighbors. Somebody had to have heard something. You can't suppress a heavy round the way you can a twenty-two."

"It was a game day, don't forget. If the Wolverines won, they might have been out celebrating."

"They did. Those that stayed home might have been distracted by all the shouting and horn-honking. They don't set fire to cars here, not as a rule, but it can get pretty rowdy. Still, a heavy caliber going off in the middle of student housing—" He shook his sleek head.

"Yeah, they built these places cheek by jowl."

He got up, looking dour all over his broad Slavic face. "Well, you can dance in the end zone: found your clients' man between lunch and supper. I don't guess you guaranteed them against damage, even if they're not dirty. Now hit the showers and let the home team mop up. And don't tell anyone what you saw in Marcus' movie."

I blew a stuttering stream of smoke, screwed out the butt against the sole of my shoe, and dropped it into a pocket. "I wasn't expecting the sundown speech. I had you pegged for the 'Don't leave town' type."

"We'll need your statement tomorrow. After that, come back anytime. Spring's good. We're proud of our trees."

"I still have to report."

"Sure. Just remember what I said about the movie. It'll spoil the ending."

And then damned if he didn't shake my hand.


I'd been run out on rails a lot less comfortable. He had breaking-and-entering against me if he wanted to lean—pushing open a door, even an unlocked one, is enough—but I'd given him a head start of a day or two before the neighbors complained about the odor, so we were square. In homicide, a day or two this way or that can make all the difference. I'd even given him a lead. I felt so gooey I thought I'd pay the fresh ticket I found on my windshield.

I walked a block over to the student union building, a brick pile built during the Gilded Age, when the corruption was honest and open. It was as likely a place to find a phone as any. A broad staircase led to a former ballroom on a second floor done in marble and golden oak. I walked right past a row of varnished doors with beveled-glass panes, then went back and swung one of them open. Inside I sat on upholstered leather and placed my first completely private call from a public convenience in years. Dante Gunnar answered.

"Hold on. I'll get her."

When Heloise came on, I told her about Jerry Marcus, leaving out the address where I'd found him and that I'd seen the Gunnars' car on his video. For a few seconds I didn't hear anything on her end, even ambient noise. She was relaying the information to her husband with her hand cupped over the mouthpiece. Then:

"Are the police sure it wasn't an accident?" She sounded as if I'd told her she needed new tires. You can't tell anything from her type.

"It's possible he shot himself cleaning his own gun," I said. "Getting rid of it afterwards and climbing in with the ironing board takes more doing. The cops think someone will come forward with information. You couldn't park a bike between those houses."

She fell for that like a piece of goose down. "What houses? You didn't say where it happened."

"Is it important?"

"I suppose not. Did you find the money?"

"I didn't look. The job was to find Marcus, not the fifteen grand."

The temperature on her end dropped twenty degrees. It hadn't been anything to bask in under normal circumstances. "Since you found him in one day, we'll expect a check for the other two. Minus your expenses, of course.

I'm sorry if that sounds cold. As Dante said, we aren't so comfortable we can take a loss like this without it hurting."

I listened to the dial tone and hung up. She sounded sorry; and I sound just like Harry Connick, Jr. in the shower. It didn't make her a murderer.

I remembered past promises. I got the *Ann Arbor News* features editor on the line and sketched the picture, without the Volvo and without the Gunnars. She could get them from the cops.

"My, my," she said. "We're getting to be quite the big city. Our police reporter's there now, as a matter of fact; he heard it on the scanner, only without those details. If you'll let me quote you, he and I can share the byline. You can only write about so many juggling grandmothers before you forget why you got into this racket in the first place."

"Tell your readers I get fifteen hundred up front. Juggling grandmothers welcome."

The job was finished, and if it wasn't the record, it was close. Finding a corpse earned an asterisk at least. Another day, another five hundred dollars, less two parking tickets. Much as I'd have liked to have fobbed them off on my clients, it wouldn't be fair just because I didn't like them. It wasn't worth what I'd find at the bottom of that slippery slope.

I cranked the Cutlass out of its slot, this time ahead of the meter maid, joined the lockstep traffic downtown, and took the expressway home, where homicide is just something the hacks use to separate sports from weather.

The story made the second half of the TV news. Murder mysteries sell advertising, and roving reporters always like a change of scenery. Lieutenant Karyl—the legend at the bottom of the screen said Alexander was his first name—shrugged them off, referring them to headquarters for details. He looked twice as broad across the shoulders on the tube.

I mixed a drink, stretched out in my armchair, and started a book; noticing for the first time that I was reading these days at arm's length.

# SIX

The *Free Press* had more details the next morning.

Heloise and Dante had been questioned and released, by reason of a plausible alibi: The medical examiner had placed Jerry Marcus' death between 3:00 and 7:00 P.M. Saturday, when Michigan was hosting Northwestern at the Big House on Stadium Boulevard, and witnesses had placed the couple at a fund-raiser for the Green Party candidate for county commissioner at the Ann Arbor Country Club, twenty minutes away from Thompson Street by automobile, all that afternoon.

A Volvo answering the description of theirs showing up in the dead man's film didn't make it into print, so either the cops had been satisfied on that point or they hadn't been able to work it into the puzzle yet. One of those trees the city was so proud of had obscured the license plate, and anyone can buy the same bumper stickers they had. That wasn't enough for any cop, if he believed what I remembered about their placement and it matched the video, but any competent defense lawyer could cut that up for stew meat.

I got my statement out of the way early. The city police operated out of a low orange-brick building on Fifth Street, two blocks east of Main. It looked like a high school, except for a few more blue-and-whites in its parking lot. Karyl wasn't in. The young black plainclothesman who interviewed me for a video camera was polite; when he went back over some details I'd already supplied, he apologized, and it seemed genuine. Afterward we exchanged cards. He was interested in moonlighting as a private investigator, if the department would let him. I was back on the road by noon.

Driving home I thought about the case. It was the cleanest break I'd ever made from one with a body in it. Loose ends are a part of life, like lumpy mashed potatoes.

I don't like either, but then I have more time to poke at them than the police. The car thing kept coming back, along with the mental picture of Jerry Marcus' cramped resting place in his shabby little room off campus. I couldn't work Heloise or Dante into that. Confronting a possible con artist is one thing, forcing him to the floor and putting a slug through his brain another. Their support for gun control could have been a blind; but the way the thing had gone down didn't fit a couple who thought the Young Republicans were a dangerous cult. Their method would have been to spike his herbal tea with 100 percent vegetable alkaline.

That cardboard box bothered me too, the one the skinhead girl on the porch had seen Marcus carrying out to his car the day he was killed. Karyl hadn't seemed to think much of it; but from what little exposure I'd had to the lieutenant, I knew he hadn't forgotten it. He was a human vacuum cleaner if ever there was one.

Rosecranz, the Russian cocktail who kept my office building from falling into a heap of asbestos, was riding a buffer as big as he was over the linoleum in the foyer. I missed the point. You couldn't raise a shine there with a séance. I figured he had millions in pre-revolutionary rubles stashed in a hollow tree in Gorky Park and was just biding his time until he could go back and retrieve it. I gave him a thumbs-up in passing, just to keep me in his thoughts. He tugged at the lobe of an ear the size of a cabbage and went on buffing. I couldn't be sure, but I thought it made us comrades.

I ran square into a spiderweb on the way through the door of my office. I'd been gone only a day. Until then I'd thought I was a fast worker.

A patch of rug, a desk, some file cases, Chief Crazy Horse skunking Custer in a beer advertisement on the wall: the place where a thousand mysteries came to roost. Not the place I sleep, but home just the same. I checked my service, but the cool female voice said I hadn't been popular lately. There were days when she was my only human contact.

I sat in the swivel, made out a check for a thousand dollars, less gasoline, toll calls, and the beef and cheddar at the deli, and mailed it to the Gunnars along with a one-page typewritten report. Once again I left out the part about their car. For all I knew the cops were still sitting on that one, waiting for it to hatch.

After that I smoked a cigarette and wondered if it was too early to break the bottle out of the safe.

Instead I picked up the receiver and tried the last-number-dialed I'd gotten from Marcus' telephone. I hadn't told Karyl about that; he'd have thought of it himself, and wouldn't be any too pleased that I had and had acted upon it. It was bad enough I'd used the phone to call 9ll. That could be dismissed as a lapse in judgment, not obstruction of justice.

One of those canned announcements that come with the answering machine—no identification of any kind—asked me to leave a message. I thought about calling on Barry and his reverse directories, but I slapped the back of my hand.

Done is done. *John* Donne: "No man is an island." Says who? Simon and Garfunkel: "I am an island." If you know the Bible well enough you can argue any case. I bent to the safe.

Soon, though, I hadn't time to do anything else, even the office bottle. I'd scored some insurance work for a company whose client may or may not have arranged to have his 2000 GMC Sonoma stolen and set afire in a weedy lot near the Michigan Central tracks, and between interviewing witnesses and taking pictures of the garage the client said someone had broken into and canvassing the neighbors, my little tin office was just a place to rest my jaw and my feet. Three days of that, and all I had was dead certainty the client was a fraud, and as much of a chance of proving it as Rosecranz had of seeing his face in the linoleum in the foyer.

Who cares? Not the insurance company, or even the other clients who covered the bill; a few pennies more on the premium. What business was it of mine if some schnook got behind in his payments and took care of the problem with two bucks' worth of gas and a penny match? Big corporations do it all the time, on a much larger scale. What was I, a Communist? Not a bit. You go into a thing with justice in mind and finish up putting the screws to a guy who if you were in his place you might do the same thing.

Nope. Crooked is crooked. I slid what I had into an envelope and threw it on the OUT stack under the mail slot. Someone else would have to build a rock-solid case out of kindling.

Other things were in the fire. Some people still preferred to do credit checks through a professional agency rather than the Internet, where whales and dolphins were reported to migrate through the Great Lakes, Moby Dick waiting patiently for the locks to fill between Superior and Huron. Purely as a courtesy to an old flame, I set aside a career-long policy of not accepting divorce cases, only to find that the stockbroker husband was shoveling coke into the ovens at the Ford River Rouge plant to cover his losses on the New York Stock Exchange, and not spending his evenings with his teenage intern; I gave her that one on the house for old times' sake. I shot video of a chronic back injury doing the chicken dance at his cousin's wedding reception, then erased it. I could do a mean lambada myself with an open bar at my elbow. The company settled, and said it wouldn't be needing my services in the future.

So it's not all waterfront liaisons, running gun battles on fire escapes and across rooftops, Arab princesses trading places with their handmaidens to see how the other half died. I went weeks at a time with nobody shooting at me or coldcocking me with a sap or shanghaiing me into the hold of a tramp steamer bound for Singapore, or even Sioux Falls. There were times when the trench coat and fedora languished so long at the cleaners someone considered donating them to the shelter for retired private detectives; gray men with bunched chins, sitting in their wheelchairs staring at the wall, fingering the pulp at the back of their heads, and calling the nurses dames and tomatoes: *There, there, Mr. Rockhammer. Swallow what's in this plastic cup and tell yourself it's rye. There's a good little shamus. Nighty-night, and don't let the femmes fatales bite.*

It's a job, not a crusade. Crusades are for martyrs, and we know what happens to martyrs. They wind up nailed to a cross or burned at the stake or bristling with arrows or fed to lions or having their intestines unwound from their insides with a windlass; which was my favorite. Modern-day villains have no imagination. Throwing a guy down on his face and putting an ounce of lead through his brain is for pussies.

I was back behind the desk stapling together a sheaf of affidavits when Heloise Gunnar called.

"Thank God," she said; "not that I believe there is one. I've been trying to reach you all day."

It was the first sign of emotion I'd heard in her voice. A

carved head on Easter Island could have sneezed and I'd have been too surprised to say gesundheit. Ice cubes collided in a glass far away. I didn't think they were floating in turnip juice.

"You should've left a message," I said. "I'd have called back."

"I didn't know what message to leave. I didn't know who'd be listening. I didn't know who I could trust. Can I trust you?"

"If you don't know the answer to that question, it's dangerous to ask." I went on stapling; or my hand did. That was one collection of papers that would stay together longer than the Stones.

"*Please!*"

That tore it. When an iceberg spews lava, you stop what you're doing and concentrate. I laid aside the pages and stapler and took the receiver out of the crook of my shoulder. "What kind of trust do you need, Ms. Gunnar?"

"The attorney-client kind, if you can give it. My husband's been arrested for murder."

"*Dante?* They'll kick him before dark. He wouldn't kill a fly even with kindness. He'd apologize for interrupting it before it finished buzzing."

"That's just it." She spoke so low I had to screw the receiver into my ear to make it out. "I'm not sure it's a mistake."

# SEVEN

It was one of those houses you see perched on the tall hills looking down on Huron River Drive, the ones you catch glimpses of from below when the leaves thin out, a patch of siding here, a flash of glass there. The trees were as green and as fat as artichokes, so the first clue I was getting close came when I entered a sharp curve and a diamond-shaped sign leapt out of the bushes reading HIDDEN DRIVEWAY. The two-lane blacktop is a crazy serpentine scenic highway following the bank of a tributary of Lake Huron, a trade route for all the tribes and traders in the old Northwest Territory. LaSalle, Cadillac, and Pontiac had navigated it, long before their names were etched in chrome. When I downshifted for the turn, I couldn't be sure if the canoe I thought I spotted was there or if it was paddled by ghosts. I pushed my old Cutlass up a twisting stretch of black composition flanked by cedars hanging on by their teeth.

At length it flattened out and drew a loop in front of a

big Tudor with three sharp gables sticking up like the points of a display handkerchief. There was a four-car garage attached and a satellite dish on either end of the roof. Offhand it looked like Dante could have blown off that fifteen g's like a white chip, but any lifestyle is possible in the age of the thirty-year fixed mortgage; for a while, anyway.

Heloise answered the door herself in a purple caftan robe with her bare toes sticking out under the hem. Her straight graying hair needed brushing and there was a thumb-size smudge on her rimless glasses. Half-melted ice cubes bobbed in clear liquid in a tall glass in her right hand. She shifted it to the left to take mine in a surprisingly warm grip.

"Thanks so much for coming. Did you have any trouble finding the place?"

"I turned into a couple of wrong driveways. If I'd known how far the addresses are from the road I'd have brought along the Hubble telescope."

She led me into a ground floor that was really a balcony encircling a conversation pit, with carpeted steps leading down into it. There was a fireplace that looked as if it were made of black glass, a marble shin-buster of a coffee table, and contemporary seating upholstered in slate leather. Copies of *Mother Jones* and the *Ann Arbor Observer* were fanned out on the table.

"Amos Walker, this is Hernando Suiz, our attorney."

I shook the hand of the fiftyish man standing inside the pit. He wore his salt-and-pepper hair in a brush cut and a summerweight suit the color of the Mediterranean at midnight, or how it ought to; the Gulf of Tonkin was as close as I'd ever come. The whites of his eyes glistened against brown skin. He was shorter than he appeared and not as friendly as his smile.

"I'm glad you wanted me present," Suiz said, "although I'm a little surprised. Had Mrs. Gunnar confided to me her plans, I'd have advised her against calling you."

"She wanted attorney-client privilege. I can't offer that unless she hires me through an attorney. I'm pretty good at keeping the lid on, but if the cops jail me for withholding information, I can't be much help."

"Are you afraid of going to jail?"

"You wouldn't ask that question if you'd ever gone. All things being equal, I'd choose walking barefoot on broken glass; a little alcohol and gauze and it's all over in a day. In either case I'm no good to anyone while it's in process."

He smoothed a lighter-than-air lapel. "I wasn't aware Mr. and Mrs. Gunnar existed before this morning, so of course your name meant nothing. I made some calls. My grassroots poll puts you at fifty-fifty friends to enemies."

"I'd rather you hadn't done that," I said.

"Because you knew it wouldn't come out in your favor."

"Because it's like someone checking your credit rating: Every hit knocks you down a point. Come the time I'll need those references, they figure time spent as opposed to time earned, and I'm left twisting on account of I'm not worth the effort. But I can't help thinking, since you and I are talking, that I gained some ground."

Heloise slammed ice cubes from a bucket into another tall glass on the table. "Sit down, please. We haven't time for these male rites while Dante's in jail." She filled the glass from a decanter and stuck it in my hand.

She hadn't offered, and I hadn't asked. I didn't care for the stuff as a rule; people who drink vodka straight up don't like drinking. Oblivion is the object. I sipped it anyway. It was going to be that kind of meeting. A full glass stood untouched in front of Suiz. We'd drawn our lines in the sand. I told Heloise she had a beautiful house.

"Thank you. We're subletting it from a professor of Medieval Studies while he's in Spain." She refilled her glass without disturbing the ice in the bucket. "We gave up our apartment downtown. Traffic was horrible on a day-to-day basis, and four days each summer we were prisoners of the art fairs. There are too many people in the world, and far too many cars. You know the police have a picture of our car parked near the murder house." She sat.

"That's not evidence," I said. "Anyone can park his car anywhere, so long as he doesn't park it illegally, and that's just a misdemeanor. There's no law against parking it in front of a murder scene."

"You have a sound layman's knowledge of the law," Suiz said. "Lord knows there are only so many spaces in this town. I myself choose the side streets, hoping to find a slot ten or twelve blocks from my destination, even more by choice, sometimes; I like to keep fit." He smacked a stomach as lean as ground round.

I looked at Heloise. "They're holding your husband on what charge?"

"Suspicion of homicide." She shuddered at the phrase.

"The arraignment's tomorrow. Bail won't be set until then." She inhaled an ounce of pure grain alcohol. "I may be arrested too, for filing a false statement."

"One moment." The lawyer leaned forward. "Until we've engaged Mr. Walker's services, everything we say here is evidence."

"Have you got it?" I asked Heloise.

Her face went vacant. I wondered how much she'd had to drink before I'd arrived. I'd had her down for another helping of mineral water, with a dash of bitters when she felt adventurous. Then she thrust a hand into her robe pocket and brought out a crumple of paper.

"Give it to Mr. Suiz," I said.

The lawyer took it from her gently. He stretched it between both hands. After a beat he nodded and thrust it toward me.

It was a check made out in my hand to the Gunnars, in the amount of the retainer I hadn't earned.

I pocketed it. "I'm on the defense team now. If the cops put the screws to me, I'll let Mr. Suiz off the leash." I looked at him. "If that's not how you see it, I'm off the case."

A muscle worked in one brown cheek.

"I can't say I appreciate the metaphor; but I admire your layman's grasp of criminal law."

"Is that a yes? I gave up trying to speak lawyer years ago."

He sat back. "Yes."

I looked at Heloise. "What did you tell the police?"

A pair of eyes marinated in pure grain alcohol floated my way behind rimless lenses.

"I said Dante was at my side at the country club all Saturday afternoon. That wasn't strictly true." She drew her right hand up her right arm, elbow to shoulder, then back down.

"I doubt they'll arrest you," Suiz said, "although they may apply it as leverage to force you to testify against Mr. Gunnar."

She sat up straight, splashing liquid from her glass. "But they can't!"

"They can, if you turn state's evidence to save yourself." Suiz's tone was deadly calm. "You must face it, Heloise. You're in this for yourself. Do you think Dante would hesitate to implicate you to save his own skin?"

I made a time-out gesture. "Who are you representing, counselor? Mrs. Gunnar hired you to defend Mr. Gunnar."

We were seated in the conversation pit, Heloise and I on a couch upholstered in tough yellow Naugahyde, Suiz in an Eames chair. He subsided into leather and down. He ignored me, addressing Heloise.

"I doubt they'll arrest you, although they may apply the threat of it as leverage to force you to testify against your husband, regardless of the law against it; *force* as a psychological term is open to interpretation. The police play childish games, as transparent as they are cruel, but they know what they're about."

Heloise looked at me. It was as if Suiz hadn't spoken.

"The truth is, I lost track of Dante several times during the fund-raiser. You have no idea of what goes on at those things. Later, the police talked to the people who were there. Most of them said I was present the whole time, Dante, too, but of course I excused myself to go to the bathroom once or twice, and I doubt anyone timed how long I was gone. I'm sure it was the same with Dante. I mean, who pays attention? Everyone has a life."

She took a long draft from her glass. "It's just possible Dante slipped away long enough to—kill Jerry Marcus, and return to the club without anyone noticing he'd been gone. The drinking, the too-loud conversation, the god-damn band—the fucking band, 'Don't go changin',' for chrissake—" She threw another slug on top of the last. Bad music and strong alcohol went together like beer and pretzels.

I looked at Suiz. "What else have they got?"

"I spoke with a lieutenant named Karyl. He's much more certain of his suspect than he is of his case. He has a mo-tive: Mr. Gunnar thought Marcus cheated him of fifteen thousand dollars he and Mrs. Gunnar had invested in his independent film, a science-fiction thriller to be shot en-tirely in Ann Arbor, employing local actors. Karyl hasn't found the weapon, a nine-millimeter automatic pistol—"

I broke in. "Tech on the scene thought it was a thirty-eight, or a three-fifty-seven Magnum."

"I'm a criminal attorney," Suiz said stiffly. "A lot of things get said on a crime scene that don't hold up in the lab. To be fair, it's a matter of a few grains on the scale. Either way it's a big enough caliber to put a serious hole through anyone's plans for the future, yes?"

"Don't badger me, counselor. How many times I've been shot is my business."

He backed off, lowering his lids over the whites of his eyes.

"So no murder weapon yet, but Karyl has opportunity, thanks to the confusion at the country club, and a bit of film Marcus shot showing what may be the Gunnars' automobile parked in front of Marcus' place of residence, indicating although not proving he knew where to find him. I understand you supplied that intelligence."

"They'd have found it out soon anyway. I've got a license, just like you. What else?"

"There's nothing else. Gunnar's clammed up on my advice. If they had any case at all they'd go after *Mrs.* Gunnar as an accomplice before and after the fact. And they have a whopping loose end that can destroy them in court."

"Jerry Marcus' yellow Mustang."

All the air went out of him then. He'd tagged me for a gum sole and the brain of a draft horse, and I knew he'd never forgive me for disappointing him on that issue.

I lit a cigarette, depositing the match in a pottery dish on the coffee table. I didn't want it especially, just the pause for devastating effect. Outside, a cricket yawned and scratched its butt. "The last witness who saw him alive told me she saw Marcus load what looked like a toaster-oven box into an old yellow Mustang and drive away. No vehicle answering that description was parked anywhere near the house when I found the body."

Suiz produced something the size of a pinochle deck from a pocket and thumbed some buttons.

"Holly Zacharias," he said. It sounded like an oath. "Undergraduate at the University of Michigan. She lives in a dormitory on campus. Police found a Mustang registered to Marcus burned out on a country road north of town. They think Mr. Gunnar drove his Volvo to within walking distance of Marcus' house, walked the rest of the way to avoid having his car seen in the neighborhood at the time of the murder, and drove the Mustang back to where he'd parked. They think he left the keys in the ignition and some obliging joyrider came along and stole it. Very convenient—for a mastermind."

"No mastermind would have hired me to find Marcus after he'd already driven his car to Marcus' house once," I said. "Even if he didn't know Marcus had it on film, he had to have known someone might have seen it and remembered. What's Gunnar's story?"

Suiz shook his head. He looked as heartbroken as any lawyer ever could, if any lawyer had a heart and you could break it with a sledge.

"I don't know. He won't confide. He's being foolish."

"First he's a mastermind," I said. "Now he's foolish. The middle ground? Guilty as hell."

Heloise moaned and fell off her chair, out cold.

# EIGHT

Heloise Gunnar's body barely had time to make a thud when Hernando Suiz threw himself out of his chair, dropped to his knees, and put an ear to her breast.

"She's alive, thank heaven," he said. "She fainted."

"Let's say that." I picked up the glass she'd dropped and stood it next to the half-empty decanter of clear liquid on the coffee table. She was snoring by then, loud enough to drown out a block plant, and filling the air with fumes; the same guy who'd sold Ann Arbor a bill of goods about being the cultural center of the world had started the rumor about vodka being undetectable on the breath.

I took her arms, the lawyer her feet, and we stretched her out on the slate-colored sofa. Suiz unhooked her glasses from the ear they dangled from and folded them on the table. "Should we do anything?"

"We could shove a dish towel in her mouth, but she might suffocate."

"I *meant,* should we call a doctor?"

"Let her sleep. In the morning she'll have Whitney Houston screaming in her head, but no one ever died of it."

"What makes you an expert?"

"The last time I was in a bar during happy hour, I woke up in the middle of a cockfight in Tijuana. Let's find someplace where we don't have to yell."

We ascended from the conversation pit and found a stainless-steel kitchen with granite counters and a cluster of copper pots hanging like a chandelier from the ceiling. Here, Mrs. Gunnar's snoring sounded as gentle as pounding surf. I asked Suiz if he thought Dante Gunnar had killed Jerry Marcus.

"We haven't met yet; for some reason he refuses to see me. But whether he did it isn't my concern. Mine is whether the Washtenaw County prosecutor's office can prove it. Without a murder weapon or a witness or evidence to place him at the scene, they'll have to release him."

"We won't know there's no weapon until we toss the house."

"We can't do that without Mrs. Gunnar's permission."

"By the time she sleeps it off the place could be crawling with cops."

"I'm an officer of the court," he said. "I'm bound to report it if we find anything."

"Better you know it now than in discovery."

I took the second floor, he the basement. There was nothing under the king mattress in the master bedroom, nothing in the drawers or on the top shelf of the walk-in closet that belonged in an evidence room. I went through the pockets of all the clothes hanging there and came up with a handful of fluff and a ticket stub from a Springsteen concert. The guest bedroom was even less enlightening; the closet and drawers were empty. I figured they didn't play host often. No arsenal in either bathroom or in the attic, accessed by a pull-down hatch and ladder. I caught up with Suiz while he was pulling the cushions off the love seat in the sunken living room. We exchanged a wry look over the snoring woman on the sofa and off-loaded her to the love seat to frisk the sofa.

When we finished with the kitchen, I fetched the decanter and poured two inches apiece in two water tumblers. We sipped from them facing each other in the breakfast nook.

"They'll just say he threw it in the river," I said. "He's still their number one till they get a better offer. I want to talk with him."

"He won't talk to me. Why should your luck be better?"

"If my luck were any good I wouldn't be groping through people's underwear drawers for a living," I said. "Mostly I'm sneaky. Being a lawyer you wouldn't know anything about that."

For the first time his face showed something stronger than chronic disapproval.

"Okay, I'm a shyster, a mouthpiece, a spring expert; I'd represent the devil himself for a share in hell. When I prove a cop's a crook on the stand I twisted his words. A sweet young thing lies through her teeth in front of a jury and I have to handle her with oven mitts or the jury thinks I'm a bully, so I have to call someone who can refute her, only he looks like Charles Manson and 'fuck' is the only adjective he knows, so I'm better off not having called him at all. When I win a case I slipped one past the panel, and when I lose it's because I'm incompetent. People watch Court TV and suddenly they're experts. A few years ago, a high-profile defendant in a rape case was acquitted for lack of evidence and the network reporter covering the case called it 'a flaw in the system.' Lady, that *is* the system. I put myself through law school working in a laundry, shaking maggots out of sheets and tablecloths, and it took me six years because they were both full-time jobs. The Michigan Bar exam's one of the toughest in the country; I aced it, only to spend another six years doing pro bono work for a storefront firm in Grand Rapids. I've been with my present firm fifteen years, been passed over for a partnership twice, and they tell me I have to wait for the senior partner to die before I get another shot. The senior partner's forty-two years old, plays tennis five days a week. I cry every time I lose, and when I win I'm too tired to celebrate. So I go home and flop down in front of *The Tonight Show* and listen to lawyer jokes that if they were about black people or women, the comedian would be arrested for committing a hate crime. And I'm the guy he'd call to represent him, because I'm sneaky."

"Finished?" I said.

He touched a folded handkerchief to his upper lip. "Finished. Sorry I went on."

"Don't be. It was wasted on me, for what it's worth. If it weren't for lawyers I'd be doing bodyguard work. I remem-

ber that rape case. The reporter's a Washington corre-
spondent now."

"Serves the bitch right." He returned the handkerchief
to his pocket and fussed with it until it stood to attention.
"I'm going to make the case that Gunnar isn't a flight risk
and try to get him released on his own recognizance. I feel
sure I can at least get him out on bail. You can meet with
him then, if he agrees."

"What'll they use for money? She runs a bookstore and
he's a cubicle rat for the university. When the owner of this
place gets back from Spain, it's back to an efficiency apartment for them."

He looked wry again. "It's back to pro bono for me, as
a favor to a partner. He's representing the bookstore in a
suit to shield its records from the Patriot Act. He's a dedi-
cated civil libertarian." He frowned. "I'm fairly certain this
is a nonsmoking house."

I shook out the match I'd used to light the cigarette and
got up to wash it down the drain. I switched on the exhaust
fan above the stove. He watched the smoke slither toward
it, then broke a long tan cigar out of a leather case shaped
like a rack of ribs and stuck a butane lighter under it.
It smelled of Old Havana. You can get anything in Ann
Arbor, and to hell with the embargo.

"I wouldn't read anything into Dante's silence," I said.
"He opened his mouth exactly twice the first time we
talked, the second time to bellyache about the fifteen grand
he'd paid Marcus for a share in his movie. If he killed him,
he'd have made some effort to get it back. The place was a
mess, but it hadn't been ransacked. Also I don't see him

for an execution-style murder. When I say I'm a good judge of character, it's not idle boast. I've been thirty years developing it."

"What do you suggest as an alternative?"

"Either his luck's worse than mine or he's in some kind of frame. I'm still curious about that toaster-oven box this Holly Zacharias saw Marcus take out to his car the night he was killed. People don't remember everything they saw right away. I want to ask her more about it. What was in it may tell me something."

"I doubt it."

"Me, too; but I've never been good at sitting on my hands."

He clamped the cigar between his teeth and went into conference with his electronic pocket reminder. When he gave me the bald girl's number I wrote it in my low-tech notebook, lifted the receiver off a wall extension with a brushed-aluminum finish, and dialed. I spoke with two giggling intermediaries before a voice I recognized came on.

"The detective dude." She sounded mellow. She'd progressed from beer to something stronger. "Naughty, naughty. You're no cop."

"Next time don't assume." I asked if we could meet.

"I'm late for work, but I'm off at two. I'm a waitron at the Necto."

"What language is that, Frangi?"

"I push liquor in a nightclub. It's on East Liberty. Ask anyone in town."

I looked at my watch. Four o'clock. Two meant 2:00 A.M.

"Past your bedtime, old-timer?"

"Mom's strict, but I'll climb down the trellis."

"Lose the suit," she said. "Last time one came in, half the customers took off out the back."

The timber of Heloise Gunnar's snoring changed as I hung up. "You might want to stash the alcohol," I told Suiz. "Somehow I don't think she's had the practice."

He puffed a smoke ring and watched it crawl toward the exhaust fan. "I suspect it belongs to the owner of the house. The refrigerator's full of Perrier."

"I thought you said you weren't sneaky."

"I didn't."

I grinned and washed the cigarette down after the match. "How far will my license bend if I invoke attorney-client privilege with the cops?"

"You're an officer of the court while you're in my employ. If they refuse to disclose anything about the case, call me." He stood and gave me a card engraved on Louis XIV stock. "What's next? You've got hours before your appointment."

"I've got twenty years on Holly. I need my beauty sleep."

I drove back home, caught two hours, then put on a black T-shirt and the jeans I wore to the Laundromat. I'd bought a pair of black Nikes and seasoned them by throwing them a couple of dozen times against the wall of my garage. I rumpled my hair and put a pair of dark glasses in my shirt pocket. I didn't think I had time to stop off and get a tattoo.

The mirror said I was a middle-aged man skipping out

for a night without the ball and chain. Just in case, I broke out the mad money and stuffed my wallet. That would make any door bouncer mistake me for Brad Pitt.

I didn't need an address; the place was lit up like a jukebox and the thump of bass set every window in the Cutlass buzzing. There was a line waiting to get in and no parking for six blocks. When I found a spot, behind a bank that had closed for the night, I took my time hiking back, but the line wasn't any shorter.

It was Goth Night; but then it would be. The clientele had hit every Halloween store in southeastern Michigan and there was enough armpit hair on display to knit a cyclone fence. The ogre at the door was built low to the ground, but bulged all over; even his triple chin had muscles. I gave him ten bucks to unhitch the velvet rope, skirted a small dance floor filled with the bobbing cast of an Anne Rice novel, and sat at a table the size of a Chiclet. The little combo plugged into the bandstand wasn't making any more noise than a six-engine jet carrying a cargo of loose ball bearings, but by the time a server appeared, my eardrums had grown enough callus to stop the bleeding.

"Detective dude! Looking less Republican. Last call."

Strobes shot across the surface of my shades, but I recognized Holly Zacharias' mown head and the metal glittering on her face. A black jersey sheath hung straight down from her bare shoulders to the floor, where the hem splashed out in shards. She'd painted dark circles under her eyes and was holding up a tray of drinks. Now I knew where she got that rasp; shouting over that din would raise blisters on a slide trombone.

I shouted back that I was on the wagon and asked her to join me. She fished a cell phone from between her breasts, checked the time, shrugged, parked the tray on a vacant table, and plunked herself down in the chair opposite. A bouncer built like the chunk at the door, only extruded to six-and-a-half feet, gave me the hard eye from under a mop of peroxided bangs. I always bring out the worst in people who can cause me the most physical harm.

# PART TWO

# CUTAWAY

# NINE

They closed down the Necto years ago; not for what happened that night, but for what happened on too many others. The combination of too many amateur drinkers, an overheated box of a room, and bad music provides its own brand of spontaneous combustion.

In a little while the lights came up, obliterating the purple twilight, and the patrons fled like startled bats. The band pulled the plugs on their instruments and started putting them away in cases. Impossibly youthful employees drifted through, scooping up glasses and bottles and dumping ashtrays, looking like players in a high school production of *The Rocky Horror Picture Show*. One, squatter than Humpty Dumpty at the door but all suet, garters on his chubby legs, didn't look old enough to sling drinks; but then I got the impression it wasn't the only law the Necto regarded as a polite suggestion. The lumpy surfer-haired bouncer cracked his knuckles and yawned. Goth Night was history.

"Can I have one of those?"

I looked at the girl over the pack of cigarettes I was playing with. At 2:00 A.M., under the eight-ball haircut and behind the studs and Vampira makeup, she looked as fresh as spring water. I felt like rusty trickle from the faucet, and I'd had a nap.

"How old are you?"

"Old enough to play with matches. Teen smokers keep you up nights?"

"They're shooting each other in school hallways. I don't care if they smoke." I dealt us each one and lit both. She squirted a jet at the ceiling without inhaling; she was addicted to the idea, not the tobacco. I felt a little less guilty then about her lungs. Sure, I cared. Refusing a request was no way to start an interview.

In that light I realized she was an attractive young woman. If she grew her hair out a little she'd have a Jamie Lee Curtis thing going on. The name would mean nothing to her, or anything else that predated the precise moment of her birth. The world never seemed to run out of lost generations.

"Tell me about that box you saw Jerry Marcus carrying to his car Saturday."

"You stayed up past your bedtime for that? It was a box, Bee-Oh-Ex. Picture of some tacky appliance on it. One of those counter jobs no one really needs. Dude, our world's gonna turn into one big landfill long before global warming gets us."

"It's a toaster oven, not Al-Quaeda."

"Who said it was a toaster oven?"

"You did. Are you changing your story?"

"Shit. Stop talking like the Man. You're going to dress like us, act the part." She shot another blank at the ceiling. "Could've been a baby microwave. Something I'll never have. I eat my veggies raw."

"How was he carrying it?"

"On his head, like those women on the Exploration Channel. Where you think? In his hands."

"High? Low? Did it look like it had something heavy inside?"

"You mean like Jerry's head? I didn't see anything about that on the news."

"If you're going to ask a question every time I ask one, this is going to take a really long time."

"Okay, okay. Keep your Depends on." She squinted, scratching a fresh tattoo and playing a video from the past. "I'd say it was empty or close to it, the way he handled it, but he used both hands. He set it on the seat gentle."

"Front or back?"

"What difference—?"

"Holly!" I snapped. Murph the Surf turned his head our way while talking with the bartender, a lady shot-putter with rings on every finger, like twin sets of brass knuckles.

"Sorry. Front, passenger's side, though I don't see why it's anything."

"It isn't, except the more details you try to remember, the more come back on their own."

"You mean like hypnosis? Awesome. Now I think of it, he did seem careful about not spilling anything out the hole. You think it was dope?"

"What hole?"

"There was a big hole in the side. Didn't I say that?"

"You left that part out."

"Shit. You were right about remembering."

"You were drinking when we talked."

"Beers don't affect me. Not like Sean. Dude I was with on the porch? You could've been molesting me the whole time, he wouldn't've woken up. That's why the cops talked to me and let him walk. I just forgot about the hole. It was round, like it'd been cut out. Maybe that's where he hid his movie camera. Candid, you know?"

"Cops know about the hole?"

"If I mentioned it, I don't remember." She leaned forward, resting her elbows on the table, the cigarette leaking smoke straight up along her temple. "Maybe I need hypnotized again." She thought a lopsided smile was sexy.

"I've got underwear older than you. Focus."

A lower lip made a pout. "I don't guess it matters if I told them. They didn't seem too interested anyway."

"They're trained not to. What else did you forget?"

She laid the cigarette in a shallow tin tray to smoke itself out and folded her arms on the table. "You can take off those bogus sunglasses. You look just like Tom Cruise. Not."

I took them off and put them in my T-shirt pocket. I'd been wondering why the place still seemed dark. "Let's talk about Marcus' yellow Mustang."

"Do we have to? It's what old guys drive when they can't get any action."

"Marcus was thirty."

"Duh. I *said* old."

I jammed my stub into the tray. "Were you still on the porch when he came back in it?"

"Uh-uh. The game let out and we watched the jock lovers honk at each other and then I went back to the dorm."

"That was when, about?"

"It was getting dark. Seven, I guess; in there. I'm not really into time."

I sat back and watched the smoke from my dying cigarette climb toward the lights. My brain envied it. "The medical examiner said Marcus was killed sometime between three and seven. That makes him dead when you went home."

"Maybe he parked around the corner and walked in through the back. That game traffic's thick as snot."

"Cops found the Mustang torched on a country road. I got that from the radio on the way here. They think their suspect took it to get back to where he left his own car and someone stole it afterwards. That theory works until you picture the murderer having to look for it because it wasn't parked out front."

She rolled a bare shoulder. When she did that, the six-pointed star tattooed on it seemed to open and close like one of those folded pieces of paper with different predictions written on it. My body remembered I'd slept, but my brain knew what time it was.

"You're the detective," she said. "I don't like cop stories. I only sat down with you 'cause I've been on my feet all night. My roommates are in bed and I can't go to sleep for a long time after I get off work."

The bouncer detached his forearms from the bar and came over on the balls of his feet like a dancer. His arms bent out from his body in a loving-cup effect; pumping iron shortens the tendons.

"Closing, Holly. Tell your pickup it's time to fall out."

"Ewwwww!" I hoped she was reacting to his cologne. He'd swum two laps in it.

He leaned his knuckles on the table, bringing his face within three inches of mine. He wore braces with hinges. "You should be ashamed of yourself, mister. Ain't the women in the nursing home good enough for you?"

I used my cigarette stump to tamp out Holly's, which was still smoldering. I gave this all my attention. "Not tonight, Blondie. I get cranky when I'm up past *Matlock*. I might chastise you."

"I don't know what that means."

"'Roids." I grinned at Holly. "Shrinks 'em at both ends."

She laughed. She had one of those husky laughs you feel clear down to the floor. "Step off, Merle," she said. "They pay you to stop fights, not start them."

He straightened, opening and closing his fists at his sides. "Get your asses out of here, both of you."

I stood, put out a hand for Holly, but she was up already. I asked if she had a ride.

"I walk. It's not far." She started toward the door.

I caught up. Merle hung back by the table, burning holes in my shoulder blades. I said, "It's the short walks you don't get to finish."

"Oh, macho it down a little, Peter Parker. This isn't Detroit."

"I have to save face for Merle." I raced her for the door handle, and this time I won. "Humor an old man and tell the cops everything you told me. The more people who know, the safer the walk."

The door was open. It might have been the light from the streetlamp, but her face looked pale. "The killer, you mean. A box, that's all I saw."

"If it's more than a box, and Marcus told someone you saw it, Ann Arbor might as well be Detroit."

"You're not so old," she said. "My father's older than you and he just bought a Harley." But she kept close as we walked, with me on the gutter side.

I talked to keep her mind off the walk. "What are you studying?"

"Marine Biology. I'm gonna work at SeaWorld."

"Great job."

"Gonna hang around long enough to win their trust, then I'm gonna open the gate and let Shamu swim out to sea."

It had rained while I was inside the club. Liberty Street shone like the business side of a sheet of carbon, which was a reference Holly wouldn't get. I felt old. Water sprayed in fine mists from tires on the pavement. There's always traffic in a college town, no matter the hour. A white Crown Victoria boated into the curb. It didn't have to mean anything. People are always picking up customers when the bars close. It didn't have to mean anything; but I wished I hadn't left my .38 in the car. I hadn't known whether I'd be patted down at the door. I grasped Holly's arm firmly above the elbow.

A hand as heavy as a chain mail glove closed on my shoulder, a dozen times harder than I was holding the girl. "I'm off the clock, creep."

I bent forward at the waist, pulling Merle off balance with his hand locked on my shoulder. He wrapped his other arm around me, tight enough to make my ribs creak. I shoved Holly hard enough to take her off her feet. She was young; her bruises would heal fast. Suddenly I was supporting all the bouncer's weight. I twisted, bringing up my right shoulder and going for the snap that would send Merle into a beautiful arc above my head and land him on his back.

I heard a flat cough, the way gunfire always sounds in open air; those ear-splitting reports in the movies are dubbed in back at the studio. Holly yelled. Tires wailed, scratching for traction on wet asphalt. Then I sank under two hundred ten pounds of dead weight.

# TEN

Lieutenant Karyl's office in the brick municipal building was a perfect cube of corkboard, with a chip-and-laminate desk, telephone, fax, and computer, a tower filled with discs to back up the computer, and a two-drawer sheet-metal file cabinet to back up the discs. He was a belt-and-suspenders kind of cop.

The only thing unofficial in the room was a large framed aerial shot of the University of Michigan football stadium—the Big House, they call it—numbered and signed by the photographer, hung with levels on one wall. The whole place looked as if it had been put up by carnies and could be struck and stacked aboard a flatbed truck in five minutes flat. But they'd have to do it around the lieutenant, who sat behind the desk as solidly as an iron bell in a cathedral.

He was stuffed tightly as ever into his blue suit, and his broad Hungarian peasant's face wore no expression at all, which is as hard to bring off as a blank mind. To look at him you wouldn't know he'd gotten out of a warm bed into the chill predawn of the first day after the end of Indian summer. He said yes a couple of times into the telephone, listened without moving his face, and cradled the instrument.

"That was Saint Joseph Mercy," he told me. "Merle won't be throwing any drunks down steps for a couple of months, but he'll survive. He took one in the thigh. Missed the femoral by a centimeter."

"Must've ricocheted off a quad." I rubbed my eyes. That afternoon nap was a hundred years ago.

"We caught a break on that Crown Vic. Sheriff's deputy saw it burning on the shoulder of Ann Arbor–Saline Road and put it out with the extinguisher in his car before it was totally involved. Forensics lifted some prints off the wheel. What do you want to bet they belong to the guy who reported it stolen?"

"No bet." I yawned bitterly. I'd been up all night, shot at, helped cure two cases of hysterics—one of them mine— talked to an ambulance crew and half the Ann Arbor Police Department, and still saw nothing but Karyl at the end of the tunnel. "This torching of stolen cars is getting to be a fad."

"You'd think we were Michigan State after a big game." His brow was black and unbroken, like the space bar on a typewriter. "Whoever took Marcus' Mustang and torched it doesn't have to be the same person who shot the bouncer and set fire to the car he shot him from. You said yourself the bouncer has a personality problem, which by the way is in the job description at dumps like the Necto. Close one down, three more open up; it's like plucking gray hairs. If they didn't hire these gorillas they wouldn't need them. Maybe he was the target all along. You and the Zacharias girl just happened to be in the wrong place at the wrong time."

"That's the title of my autobiography. But I'm not buying it and neither are you."

"No, but someone had to say it. Either whoever killed Jerry Marcus thinks you're getting close or he's afraid Holly saw or heard something important around the time of the murder. It was the bouncer who had the rotten timing and the bad sense of direction."

He folded his hands on the desk; they were surprisingly fair and fine-boned, the hands of a blackjack dealer rather than the great-great-grandson of a bricklayer or stonemason; but for all I knew the old man had been a surgeon.

"If this were the Old West, I'd run you out of town. We don't get many shootings here, and we've had two just since you breezed in."

"That's the second time you gave me the sundown speech," I said. "I'm starting to think that WELCOME TO ANN ARBOR sign is disingenuous."

"Maybe if you'd told us more about that box Holly saw. She calmed down enough to tell us what you talked about in the club before we took her home."

"You shot it down the first time I mentioned it. I had the part about the hole five minutes when the fireworks came. You're going to have to do better than that if you want to make the case for obstruction of justice."

"Were you *going* to tell us?"

"She couldn't remember if she'd told you herself. She's immune to the effects of alcohol, she says. I've got my doubts. Tell me the cop who took her home has orders to stick."

The iron bell behind the desk shifted its weight. I braced for the gong.

"Who wants to know, the cradle robber or the detective? I'm asking because as far as you're concerned the case was over when you found Marcus' body."

I got my wallet out of my hip pocket and gave him Hernando Suiz's card. "That's Dante Gunnar's lawyer. He hired me to investigate the case against his client."

"I'll confirm it when he gets to his office." He parked the card in the center of the desktop. "This puts us on opposing teams."

"Not if your suspect's clean. He can't sit on a cot in the county jail and shoot a bouncer on Liberty at the same time."

"He can if his lawyer sprang him on his own recognizance yesterday afternoon."

"He moves too fast for his clients' own good." I swallowed another yawn. "You're not the stone wall you pretend to be, Lieutenant. You know Gunnar's innocent."

"I don't know that at all. That was his car parked in front of a house he supposedly didn't know existed."

"Even if you identify it definitely, Suiz will get it thrown out without opening his briefcase. There's no law against parking in Ann Arbor, as long as it's a legal spot and you don't overstay your welcome. Just between you and me it stinks, but it's not evidence."

"Let's *talk* evidence," he said. "The slug the techie dug out of the apartment floor came from a three-fifty-seven Magnum. The one the surgeon got out of Merle is on its way to the lab in Lansing. If it's a Mag round and the striations match, we've got the chance to solve two shootings at one stroke."

"Let's hope. I didn't come here to export murderers from Detroit, whatever you think."

"Go back there and get some sleep. The Zacharias girl's okay. We mean to keep her that way. She's the only real witness we've got; although what a hole in a box has to do with anything, I sure don't know."

"Jerry seemed to think it was important. So did someone else. I haven't made anybody mad lately, not counting you, and targeting Merle just when I'm working a homicide doesn't scan."

He accompanied me out into the hallway. The skeleton crew was still on and we had it to ourselves. Pinkish gray light seeped in through the windows. Nothing is colder or more hollow than a deserted government building. It's like a body without a soul; even the ghosts seemed to have gone home at quitting. Somewhere on the other side of the Milky Way a vacuum cleaner whined, a sound more monotonous than dead silence.

It was an appliance, for God's sake. I wax poetic when I go without sleep twenty-two hours out of twenty-four. My back hurt from supporting Merle's tenth of a ton and my stomach was empty to the point of pain. I hadn't eaten since lunch, and come to think of it I'd skipped lunch.

"Gunnar's not the only suspect, if that means anything," Karyl said. "Since the story broke, three more investors in Marcus' movie have come forward. He tapped one poor sucker for twenty-five thousand; that alone, on top of Dante's cut, comes to more than a hundred percent in shares, based on the budget. Only hotels and airlines can get away with selling more than a hundred percent of anything. Lucky for the sucker, he was in Florida over the weekend. The other alibis checked too.

"We got a court order and opened a safe-deposit box in Jerry's name at the Bank of Ann Arbor. It was empty. No one pays to keep a box empty, so the theory is he'd cleaned it out recently. We've put in for a warrant to search the house on Thompson. He might have stashed it in another room just in case he was targeted."

"It's a wonder he lasted as long as he did."

"This town has a soft spot for white-collar criminals. So far the U of M's accepted almost a hundred million in donations from an alumnus who went to the federal pen for insider trading."

I stopped walking, leaned against the wall, and hung a cigarette off my lower lip. "Drop the charges. You can always reboot them if you have a case. Right now Suiz is working gratis. The minute he smells a suit for false arrest and unlawful imprisonment, you'll be buried under so much paper you'll never make an arrest that will stick.

"And there's a bonus," I said. "You won't see me again until I take in the summer art fairs."

He blinked for the first time since I knew him. "Sold. If I can sell it to the brass."

A telephone rang somewhere in the building. At that hour it had a lonely sound, like the last robin of fall signing off.

"That's mine." He shook my hand again and hurried back to take the call. He was the damnedest combination of old-school and new school law enforcement I'd ever met. They would either make him chief someday or force him out as a threat to his superiors.

I was lighting up in the parking lot when he came out, moving faster than before. His face wore something like an expression.

"Good, you're still here. Saves the taxpayers the price of a long-distance call. You know Forensics ID'd Jerry based on DNA. It was him, all right. You can't buck science."

"Who's bucking it? Last time I tried I failed the course." But I wasn't sleepy anymore. Some kind of tide was coming in and I had to be ready to wade or swim.

"That was them again just now. FBI called back on the prints we lifted from that Crown Vic that shot at you last night; this morning. They belong to Jerry Marcus. Positive."

I drew in smoke and held it, letting my brain cure. It went out in a blast. "He's a better shot than I thought. Dead men usually miss by a mile."

# ELEVEN

I asked Karyl if the prints were fresh. He shook his head.

"No help there. Summer and fall were dryer than usual; this morning's rain was the first one worth measuring in weeks. Latents evaporate under those conditions. Maybe not entirely, but we wouldn't get the beauties we got if they'd been there since before Marcus was killed.

"I had to go to court tomorrow?" he continued. "I'd have to testify Jerry Marcus, a stiff we autopsied yesterday, shot a bouncer outside the Necto Nightclub five hours ago. I'm glad I don't have to go to court tomorrow."

"Me, too. You don't look like you're ready to retire."

"I love you too. One thing I have to do today is get Dante Gunnar's charges dropped. If the John Doe we've got on ice isn't Marcus, we've got no motive."

"What's your best guess?"

"We have a thriving little Wiccan community here. Ask them. Meanwhile I'll be asking the lab rats how it's possible a corpse that looked like Marcus, living in Marcus' room with Marcus' DNA, managed to sew his guts back up inside, sneak out of the cold room down at County, and steal a car."

"Still think the bouncer may have been the target?"

"Man, I don't know what I think, other than we need to put Holly Zacharias in protective custody."

"Good luck with that. You can't make her go if she doesn't want to, and she won't want to. She walks half a mile home from the club every night. If rapists don't scare her—"

"That's not so much of an issue here. This isn't Detroit."

"So people keep telling me. The last town where folks didn't lock their doors was taken apart and reassembled in the Smithsonian. If she's not afraid of rapists, I doubt a little thing like a bullet will, as opposed to sleeping on county linen. Anyway she told me she doesn't like cop stories."

"I don't either, and I'm in one." He frowned again. "There's an alternative."

I picked up. "I've got a couch."

"It's your idea, if the brass finds out. What's your home number?"

I wrote it on the back of a business card and gave it to him. He glanced at it and put it in his shirt pocket. "See she stays put, and make yourself available. I don't know what that box she saw means, or if the hole's just a hole, but it's *all* she saw, and someone doesn't want her testifying about it in court, if this thing ever results in an arrest."

"Seems to me I heard that somewhere before."

"So the department will make you chief for a day, just like one of those Make-A-Wish kids. You can even run the siren."

I took that one away with me. It was too good to leave behind.

Then I came back to the building. Nothing was open yet. In the lobby I put fifty cents on the expense sheet to tell Heloise Gunnar I wanted to talk to her husband. She was up, but sounded like a warped record. I remembered I'd left her out cold on her love seat, saturated in pure grain alcohol.

"He's sleeping. Can't you see what an ordeal he's been through?"

I looked at my watch. "He can have till noon." While she was protesting, a thought hit me bang out of outer space. My brain's always clearest when my stomach's empty. "Hold on. You said Jerry Marcus showed you some of what he'd shot?"

She'd stopped yammering. I could feel her head throb clear through my handset. "Yes, with a cutaway. That's—"

"We'll discuss that at Cannes next time," I broke in. "Did he tell you he did all the camera work himself?"

"I don't know what you mean."

I blew air at the phone, fogging the shiny steel cradle. "Do you have any of that vodka left?"

"Certainly. What do you think I am?"

"An amateur. A career drunk knows all about hair-of-the-dog. If you fix yourself a brisk one and drink it off all of a piece like Bromo-Seltzer, you'll hear the choir and your head will be as clear as an alpine stream."

"Actually, any body of water exposed to the air we've poisoned—"

"Just drink the damn booze."

She set down the receiver with a thump. I fed the slot another quarter and listened to some clinking in the ambient noise on her end. A season of silence, then:

"My goodness! I thought that was a myth spread by drunks to justify taking another drink. I never—"

"Jack Dempsey said it's possible to knock a man out, then knock him back awake. He said that's how he lost the Tunney fight."

"What*ever* are you talking about?" Her voice was strong, and as dripping with disapproval as during our first meeting. It was better than making small talk with the ghost of Kurt Cobain.

"Just that you can drink yourself sober. Did Marcus tell you he did all the camera work himself?"

"I don't know that he'd done it all himself," she said. "I just assumed."

"He had a poster and some books on film in his room, but no motion-picture equipment. Those other things could have been props, bought to impress people when he had enough seed money to rent a respectable-looking office, which would help him squeeze more from the pigeons. I'm not using 'pigeons' in a pejorative sense, Mrs. Gunnar," I said, when she took in her breath; "it's just how these people characterize their victims: things that exist for no other reason than to be plucked. But he needed bait, and the tools necessary to make it. Did he say anything at all that indicated he had a partner or an employee? Most confidence men like to create the illusion of a legitimate association. It seems less fly-by-night."

"Come to think of it, he did mention an associate. Wes? No, Les."

"Just Les? No last name?"

"Dante might know. Information Services is a kind of journalism. It's his job to get names and the correct spelling. I'm the artistic one. I saw the potential in *Mr. Alien Elect* before he did."

I said, "It looks like I'll be talking to Dante."

A breath got breathed, then another. I heard a creak. She was gripping the receiver hard enough to pop something loose. When she spoke, the warped record was back on the turntable. "We were cheated, weren't we? We'll never see a penny of that fifteen thousand dollars. Unless we sue Jerry Marcus' estate."

She hadn't heard the latest, and it wasn't my place to fill her in. I looked at a drawn face in the gleaming surface of the phone cradle; a fun house image, distorted by curvature, but I couldn't lay it all on that.

"Money's a big deal," I said. "No one knows that better than me, who's got none. But Treasury prints more every day. Think what Jerry Marcus is out. Even a cheat deserves better than a bullet in the brain."

She breathed again, deep, and let it out in a whoosh. "Of course you're right. Dante will be ready to speak with you at noon. I'll make sure of it."

———

The building was beginning to come alive; the first heels tapped linoleum, greetings murmured, the merry chime of a computer booting up, the window shades flapping open on a bright new day. I felt as bright as dead flowers in a dry vase. I used my last two quarters and caught Holly Zacharias in her dorm room. She was awake, and mean as a snake.

"There's a cop camped out in the hall!" she snapped. "What is this, house arrest?"

"Protection. I signed off on it, but the cops beat me to it. You okay?"

"Am I *okay*? I was shot at!"

"'At' is the operative word in that sentence. How sure are you that was Jerry Marcus you saw the day of the murder?"

She forgot she was mad then. She'd said she didn't like cop stories, but all God's creatures are curious.

"It was him. I'm good with faces. Why?"

"Everyone's good with faces, to hear them tell it. When was the last time you heard anyone say, 'Did you see that guy? I can't for the life of me remember his face'?"

"Well, I am. I guess I should be asking if *you're* okay. That could easily have been you that got shot. Have you heard anything about Merle?"

"You can't kill guys like Merle. You have to pump them full of cyanide, bludgeon them, strangle them, shoot them full of holes, and dump them in the Neva River, like Rasputin. He'll be back throttling patrons in no time at all, good as new."

"Half the time I don't know what you're talking about," she said. "Merle isn't as bad as you make out. He's got an old man doing life in Marquette for beating his mother to death and a sister cutting herself in a private facility. If he stops paying the bills, off she goes to Ypsi State: thorium and Edison's medicine: K-k-k-k-k-k!" It was a serviceable impression of electroshock treatments.

"I'm still hazy on how beating the crap out of me would help his sister. Anyway he was lucky, apart from standing too close to you and me. Have you got any family?"

"My parents, in Chicago. Well, Chicago and Evanston. They're divorced. What's it to you?"

"You might want to cut classes and bunk with them for a few days. It's that or county food. You may be a material witness."

"To what? I told you everything I know."

"What you know just might be dynamite."

"Well, I'm not going to call my parents. I haven't heard a word from them since I moved here. I'm putting myself through school, with what I make at the Necto and a student loan. They're too busy swinging to pay much attention to their one-and-only daughter."

"You can put up at my place."

"Yeah, right."

A thousand years of inherited female experience went into those two words.

"I'll put a padlock on your side of the bedroom door," I said. "You can rent a rottweiler. I'll pay the freight, but you'll have to walk him yourself. I might proselytize him."

"You'd do that to a *dog*?"

I had to laugh; it was better than beating myself to death with the receiver.

"You're attending one of the great universities of the world," I said. "Go to the library and look in the dictionary under *p*. I'll call you back after you've had a chance."

"Did you just give me a homework assignment?"

I laughed and hung up. I wasn't sleepy anymore. Holly was like a caffeine pill.

# TWELVE

So I was awake, and more alert than when I got in my eight hours. I went to a hotel called the Bell Tower, in the shadow of its namesake, and waited out the morning with a copy of the *Ann Arbor News* from a complimentary stack on the registration desk. Either the bombshell about Jerry Marcus being alive and homicidal had missed deadline or Karyl was holding it back. The three people claiming Marcus had conned them into investing in his movie were on the front page, with a jump to the back of the first section, and a photo of Karyl showing Marcus' empty safe-deposit box to reporters. Empty is the new full; but only if you're the press.

The point was Jerry Marcus had brought in enough revenue to make ten low-budget pictures, but had promised each investor a hundred percent of one. The clip I'd seen had been impressive enough to reel in a number of reasonably intelligent people with disposable income. I couldn't make the connection between it and the room where he'd died.

*If* he'd died. DNA said yes, fingerprints said something else. There was a zombie picture in it, if I could sell it to the kind of intellectual who knew what the hell Emerson was writing about, but didn't know a cutaway from a cutpurse.

There was a sidebar feature on the so-called murder victim's past as well: He was a North Dakota transplant with a widowed mother in Bismarck and a brother serving with the Peace Corps in Southeast Asia. The mother hadn't heard from either son in years. Gunnar was mentioned only as a suspect whose name wouldn't be released pending arraignment.

It never would, now. A much bigger story was about to break.

A paragraph in the police column announced the shooting in front of the Necto. No details were known as yet.

After a while I yawned again, wide enough to creak a hinge, got up, stamped circulation back into my right foot, and ordered a massive breakfast of steak and eggs in the hotel restaurant. I was so famished I plowed through the hash browns, setting aside the opposition of a lifetime to potatoes in the morning. I chased them with three cups of black coffee and a glass of orange juice, clearly made from concentrate; but then fresh-squeezed is just too chirpy for me at that time of day. I smoked a post-prandial cigarette and put boots on the ground.

"Hello, Mr. Walker."

Heloise Gunnar had transformed herself. She wore a yellow sundress showing off a figure I hadn't known she had, a touch of color on her cheeks and lips, and had ditched the granny glasses: I could just make out the rims of colorless contact lenses inside the mossy-green irises of her eyes. She led me into the conversation pit, just as if I'd never been; for her, I might not have. You can block anything you want given the choice. "Would you like a refreshment?"

"No thanks. Is he decent?"

She led me upstairs, walking dreamily like a character in Jerry Marcus' film. She wasn't drunk, as she'd been on vodka the last time; I figured she had a standing order at a local pharmacy. I went in alone and shut the door.

Dante sat propped up by a pillow in the master bedroom. His graying hair was more rumpled than usual, and his face looked as if a commune of hippies had moved out of it, loose and pouchy beyond his years. A gray tank top stood in for his pajamas, the cotton sunken into the gaps between his bones. He greeted me with the wan smile old men reserve for visitors they don't remember.

I drew a chair up to the bed. "Amos Walker. We met."

"I know. I'm not the idiot Heloise thinks I am."

"So you know you're a suspect in Jerry Marcus' murder."

"How could the police make such a mistake?"

"They're one for two. They know you'd been to Marcus' place before the murder. Marcus had it on film."

"On disc, actually. They tried to use it to pry a confession out of me." He pinched the bridge of his nose. His head ached, of course. Giving up one more sentence at a time would exhaust all his resources.

"If you knew where he was, why'd you hire me?"

"That was Heloise's idea. Why should I tell you what I wouldn't tell the police or even my lawyer?"

"Because you're not out yet. Someone got killed, and your country club alibi's rusted clean through. Just because their motive went south doesn't mean the cops won't find another. They're like snapping turtles; won't let go even if you chop their heads off."

"I left the country club to go home and have a drink. I had several. If you've ever attended a political fund-raiser, you know why. I can't stomach those people. They have all the fixed convictions of a human kaleidoscope."

"Did anyone see you go home?"

"Why would they? I'm invisible." He almost spat the word.

I was close to losing him. I took another tack. "Did Marcus ever mention someone named Les?"

The change of subjects struck him dumb. He'd been all set to pull the plug on the interview. "Les? I don't—"

"Your wife said he referred to him as an associate."

"Heloise is computer illiterate. I prepare the press release whenever the university makes a technological breakthrough, so I have a working layman's knowledge of the industry. LES is an acronym, not a person. It stands for Laser Electronic Substitute. The laser part's hogwash, and of course it's electronic. *Substitute* is the operative word. It means there are no human actors in his film; they're all computer-generated."

"You mean like in video games? They looked genuine to me on his own computer."

"There's something eerie about the movements, like when a silent film is played back at the proper speed, not herky-jerky like the Keystone Kops; some people like that. It's a brand-new program, and expensive. That was where our money was going, according to Marcus, the single biggest outlay of the venture, hence the biggest share of the profits. It excited Heloise. Like most people who know nothing about computers, she thinks they're a miracle of science and not just another office machine no one ever gets full use of.

"That's the charitable viewpoint," he added bitterly. "My wife is the kind of greedy anticapitalist who wants to squeak through the golden gate and yank it shut behind them."

His hands plucked at the fibers of his blanket; they seemed to be working independently. "Later, when the buzz wore off, the implications hit me. Are we so willingly plunging headlong toward making the human race obsolete? No professional actor will ever sit still for being replaced by a bunch of pixels. The Screen Actors Guild would go to court and make sure *Mr. Alien Elect* never saw the light of day."

"You should be less invisible," I said.

"Is that supposed to mean something?"

"It's the quiet ones who do the best thinking."

"An active brain isn't worth a damn thing when it comes with a cowardly streak. Are you married, Walker?"

"No."

"If you ever do, make sure she isn't stronger than you."

"Let's talk about how your car wound up in front of Jerry Marcus' house on Thompson."

I'd sprung it, catching him by surprise. He forgot to be angry.

He wrestled with the answer, or with the headache. He lost on both counts. "I saw him driving one day in that ridiculous yellow sports car. We hadn't heard from him, and I was beginning to suspect we'd been gulled. I followed. It was a spur-of-the-moment thing. People who know me would tell you I'm incapable of spontaneity. But no one really knows anyone, does he?"

I let that one drift as a rhetorical question. I'd never heard anyone say "gulled" out loud before.

"I lost him," he said; "or he lost me. I don't know if he saw me. Anyone can lose a Volvo. I drove around, looking down side streets and in driveways, and just as I was about to give up I saw it, parked next to the house. Would you mind?" He tilted his head toward the nightstand.

The water tumbler and aluminum pitcher were inside his reach, but I poured him a drink. When he took it in both hands and still managed to splash some over his chin, I knew why he'd asked me. His Adam's apple dipped down and up twice. I took back the glass before he could drop it and returned it to the table.

"I don't handle confrontations well," he said, wiping his mouth with the back of his hand. "I was just going to ask how the production was coming along. Maybe he'd say something about our money. The front door was open, so I went inside."

He fell silent. I tensed up. The world took a couple of turns before he spoke again; when he did, it was like someone ringing a loud bell.

"I lost my nerve," he said. "I stood in that shabby little living room five minutes and nobody showed. I thought about going upstairs; thought about it so hard I was surprised to find myself still standing in that room. You know, like when you're sleeping and you're cold and you dream you reached down and pulled the covers up to your chin, then wake up and you didn't. When I realized I was never going to climb those stairs, I left.

"I had no idea Marcus was outside, photographing my car."

There was still water in his glass. I drank it. I'd caught his headache.

"I never told Heloise about that visit," Dante said, "or anyone else. It wasn't my finest moment. When she suggested we hire a professional, I thought whoever it was wouldn't have any trouble walking up a simple flight of stairs.

"Don't tell her I chickened out," he added. "It's just what she needs to finish the job."

# THIRTEEN

Coming back along the winding scenic stretch of Huron River Drive I had to slow down behind an orange dump truck waddling along like a fat dog. For once I didn't mind. It gave my tired brain time to turn over. I watched a leaf here and there begin to show yellow, a deer bounding among the trees, flashes of brown coat and white tail, and replayed the rest of the conversation in my head.

"You risked a murder rap because you were afraid of what your wife would say if she found out you went to see Jerry Marcus?"

"Of course, I didn't know our car would show up on video. By the time the police told me the reason I was being held, it seemed too late. I'd never been to jail. I hope I never have to go again. It's worse than I ever dreamed."

"It doesn't get better with repetition."

"I don't claim to have thought it through. The idea of me killing *any*one was such a ridiculous notion I expected them to let me go right away. When that didn't happen, I made up my mind to tell the truth. But then Suiz got me out."

"The only reason you're off the hook now is Marcus threw the cops a curve. He killed someone in his place and found a way to rig the DNA evidence so he came out the victim. He might've gotten away with it if he hadn't gotten obsessed with leaving behind a witness." I'd told him then about his taking a shot at Holly Zacharias and getting his mitts all over the car he'd used.

"You can't falsify DNA," Dante said; "I've as much as said that in print. Unless the samples got switched."

"Not likely. I think the detective in charge of the case is straight. I know he's nobody's fool. Anyway, the hoops an outsider would have to jump through once those slides are in the system would incriminate him even worse."

We'd been speaking low. At that point his voice had dropped to a murmur. "As bad as it was, jail was the first vacation I've had from that witch in thirteen years."

"It may be the making of you."

He'd looked at me quickly, then decided I wasn't poking his cage.

"I suppose I put both of you in danger. If the police weren't concentrating on me—"

"They can't be everywhere. Let's remember who's to blame. Right now there's a young woman packing to blow town because Marcus—or whoever he is—missed. We can't count on his aim not improving next time. We'll all be better off when we know the name of the stiff the cops pulled out of that cupboard."

"Do you have a theory?"

"Not even a harebrained one. The dead man sure looked like the man in the picture you gave me from the paper."

"It was the man I gave the check to, I'm sure of that."

"If it means anything, you weren't the only fish he hooked. He paid for an empty safe-deposit box, which I'd bet anything wasn't empty until at least Saturday. That's when he set up this double to take his place on the slab and skedaddle with the swag, as we law enforcement professionals say. Except he dropped the ball."

"What sort of ball?"

I told him about the box with the hole in it.

"That's not much."

"It's getting to be; anyway, he seems to think so. Since everyone thought Marcus was murdered, the cops timed the death after Holly saw him with the box. Medical evidence of time-of-death is rarely precise. It can wobble an hour or more this way or that, depending on temperature and humidity and a bunch of other things the techs can't quite corral. Now it looks like Holly saw him fleeing the scene after the murder. Probably had another car waiting nearby, maybe the Crown Victoria he drove this morning and tried to torch later. His luck was still running sour; a county cop put out the fire before it could burn away his fingerprints."

"An empty box with a hole in it. Sounds like something from Poe."

"Who said it was empty? Holly said he handled it as easily as if it was, but also like he was afraid something would spill out the hole."

"The money? Our money? The investors', I mean."

"Any killer who's smart enough to fake scientific evidence is too smart to carry tens of thousands in cash in a box with a hole in it. I found something else in Marcus' room I'd forgotten about. I didn't think much of it at the time, but it's starting to look like that nail that lost a war."

"What did you find?"

"I need to discuss it with Lieutenant Karyl before anyone else. It's just the sort of thing cops get jealous about. Somehow I don't think it will be a surprise. He's like you: short on speech, long on brains."

He'd asked more questions, but when he saw they weren't any use wondered why I still cared about a case that should have been closed when he was released from jail.

"I'm off the clock where Suiz is concerned. I'll send him a bill. Meanwhile there's some collateral damage that needs cleaning up. The wrong person's on the run."

"The Holly girl? But—" He'd fallen back against the pillow then, closing his eyes. "We underestimated you. You ought to charge twice as much."

"I'd wind up with half as much work and twice as much trouble. What are you going to tell Heloise?"

"The truth. She'll enjoy that."

I took that as a curtain line and said good-bye to his wife at the front door. I'd miss the Gunnars the same way I miss mosquitoes in winter.

# FOURTEEN

In a party store I spent some more change calling my answering service. I still had one then; I'd still have it now if all the outfits hadn't gone into some other line of work. Now, every time someone hangs up on the machine, I figure I've lost a client. The ones who are too shy to record a message are usually upset enough not to haggle over my fee.

I was popular again. There were three messages: Hernando Suiz, the Gunnars' attorney, wanted a full report, and Lieutenant Karyl wanted to talk. Barry Stackpole had called just two minutes ago, asking me to call him back on his cell. I let them wait and ran the gauntlet of roommates to reach Holly Zacharias. She'd called her father, who'd bought her a seat on a Northwestern flight to Chicago leaving from Detroit Metropolitan Airport at 6:00 P.M. I asked who was taking her to the airport.

"Shuttle from the Campus Inn. It leaves at three-fifteen."

"That doesn't give you much time to pack."

"I don't have much to pack. I'm not into material possessions."

"Me neither, but the choice wasn't mine. I've got a car, such as it is. The driver doesn't accept tips."

"If you're offering a ride, I'm accepting. I get sick riding in buses."

I arranged to meet her at four, then called Barry.

He was driving, working the clutch and shifter on the Dodge Charger he'd had customized to accommodate his artificial leg. A slight echo told me he had me on speaker.

"That number you had me look up came with a name," he said. "The name showed up on the news. Still think there's nothing in it for me?"

"I didn't know it was a murder then. I can get all the abuse I want on someone else's dime." I slid a cigarette into the notch in the corner of my mouth.

"Give me something useful and I'll sing your praises to the angels."

"I may have something, but I have to run it out. That's why I called. Same favor as yesterday, new number."

"Shoot."

"Not one of my favorite expressions today." I gave him the number that had showed up on Jerry Marcus' redial. It didn't matter if Barry was doing ninety and had both hands on the wheel; he'd switched his photographic memory to digital while Kodak was still discussing the pros and cons.

"I got an exit coming up," he said. "Call me back in five."

I hung up and bought two bottles of The Glenlivet from the Sikh behind the counter and kept the receipt. If the

Marcus murder turned out to be nothing more than the usual run of mayhem, I'd owe Barry for his time.

His engine noise was missing when I called back. He'd parked. He drove like a maniac, but always with both hands on the wheel. "I put everything on my iPad," he said. "Searching, searching; wait." He snickered, a sinister sound coming from him. "What business can you have with Alec Moselle?"

"Don't know yet. I never heard of him until a second ago. Who is he?"

"You ought to read something more than *Fact Detective*." He gave me an address on Washtenaw Avenue in Ann Arbor.

I wrote it down. "How about a hint?"

"Bring along plenty of sunblock." He laughed and broke the connection. If he weren't my only friend I wouldn't like him at all.

I moved Alec Moselle to the bottom of the stack of mysteries for the time being and returned Karyl's call; I didn't feel like talking to a lawyer. I never feel like talking to a cop, but he was smack dab in the middle of the case that had put Holly on the run.

The female dispatcher or whatever who answered said the lieutenant was at lunch. She wouldn't say where.

"Amos Walker's the name," I said. "He left me a message."

"Oh, yes, Mr. Walker. He's at Thano's, on East Liberty."

Thano's Lamplighter belonged to a blue plastic awning

down from the Michigan Theater, a renovated movie palace with a gaudy marquee chased with electric bulbs. I
almost missed the restaurant, because one of the city's
sacred trees obscured the sign. I parked in an echoing
structure across from the downtown Borders and entered
a narrow front next to a record shop; in Ann Arbor, you
can still watch Rudolph Valentino loving up Nita Naldi on
the big screen and buy Sinatra on vinyl.

Inside was a shotgun arrangement going straight back
between a counter and a row of narrow booths. Karyl took
up all of one side of a booth facing the door. He hailed me
and I slid into the opposite seat. He was slurping Coke
through a straw from a tall plastic glass.

The sharp smell of cooking onions stung my eyes. I blew
my nose into a napkin. "Did they do an environmental im-
pact study before they opened this place?"

"Best-kept secret in town," he said. "Greektown should
serve moussaka this good." His fork cut into a square of
cheese, ground meat, nutmeg, and batter as if it were
meringue.

I'd gone there feeling more tired than hungry, but I'd
slept since I'd eaten, and the way he rolled his eyes when
he forked the morsel into his mouth would make a monk
break his fast. When a sweet-faced young waitress built
like Zorba boated over, I glanced at a laminated menu
stained all over with tomato sauce and ordered the lamb
shank and a glass of water.

"Holly turned down my offer," I said, when she'd left.
"She's moving in with her father in Chicago, where when

you get shot at you usually know the reason. I'm taking her to Metro this afternoon."

"She's not going."

I watched him scoop a pile of brown rice into his face. He was using those delicate hands for loaners while the paws he'd been born with were in the shop. I said nothing.

"She leaves," he said, "Marcus goes underground. We still don't know who the dead man in his apartment was. They tested the scientific evidence in Lansing twice and it came up Marcus every time. They can't both be Marcus. Me, I'm a print man. Prints on the steering wheel of that Crown Vic say Marcus. Marcus it is. If it's Holly he's after, we need her here, doing whatever it is coeds do now, to smoke him out."

"That rarely works out so well for the bait."

The waitress returned with my lamb shank steaming on a plate, my water, and a refill on Karyl's Coke. When we were alone again he said, "She'll have more plainclothes cops around her than the governor."

"That makes me feel better. You can always spot them by the Blues Brothers shades and Sta-Prest suits. He won't come within rifle range of her. So what's the point?"

"This coming from a middle-aged private cop who thinks dressing like Bono's opening act makes him invisible under colored lights."

I put the shades in my T-shirt pocket again. I felt grungier then. I'd gone twenty hours without a change of clothes.

That was a mistake, letting him see my eyes. He slid his fork into his plate and pushed it aside. "Don't even think about sneaking her out, Walker. I'm all hotted up to arrest *some*one."

"That's my first jail threat today."

"You don't want to test it. I'm just nailing down all the flaps," he said. "By now Marcus is running the other direction. He fired his last arrow when he missed you and Holly."

"I think you're other-estimating him, Lieutenant."

"What's 'other-estimating'?"

"Neither over nor under, just outside the normal criminal perimeters. If he was the running type, he wouldn't have risked this morning. He's working on his defense now. A good lawyer can stir up enough dust to bury attempted, but Holly can tie him to the murder."

"That box again."

I carved off a piece of lamb and chewed. It was tender, cooked with just the right touch of pink, but the chef might have made it from the picture in a grocery ad for all I tasted it. I was only eating it to keep my hands busy. My appetite was as dead as the lamb.

"I figured it out," I said. "Also why he cut a hole in one side."

"Me, too."

He fished in a side pocket. "I'm an old-fashioned cop. I let the people who know about such things monkey around with microscopes and blood spatters. DNA? Stands for Don't Nag About it. I work with evidence you can pick up and feel and sniff." He slapped something on the table between us.

I'd seen the Ziploc bag before, and the bits of white Styrofoam he'd scooped up from the murder scene. I'd handled one.

"Sheriff's deputies had a case just like it last year," he said, "in a rural community twenty miles from here. Guy snared a couple in a pyramid scheme, and when they pressed him about their money in their house, he excused himself, went outside, and came back in with a box just like Marcus', hole and everything. He'd filled it with Styrofoam peanuts, the kind that everything comes in through the mail and private parcel services, and stashed a revolver inside. Shot them each once, right between the eyes." He pointed a finger between mine and worked his thumb twice, then tapped the bag. "None of the neighbors heard the shots. That how you saw it?"

I nodded. "Any connection?"

"No. Those county cops are good. They nailed the guy in less than two weeks. It was written up, even made the Detroit TV stations. It may have been where Marcus got the idea."

"I don't remember the case, but I couldn't stop thinking about how someone could fire a heavy piece like a Magnum in broad daylight in the middle of crowded student housing, with a couple of kids swilling beer right on the front porch, and not be heard. Guns are easier to get than suppressors, and if it was a revolver—" I looked the question.

"It was. Unjacketed slug."

"Settles the point. A revolver isn't self-contained, like

a semiautomatic pistol; the noise leaks out of the firing mechanism and the cylinder, not just the barrel. But if he packed the box tightly enough with shipping material, it would sound like somebody dropping a book on the floor. Who'd remember that in Ann Arbor?" I tapped the bag. "Can you make a case?"

"The state police lab found scorching and traces of spent powder on some of the pieces, but we need more. The box is long gone, but it was his hard luck someone saw him carrying it out of the house, and remembered. He proba-bly thought she was as fogged up with beer as her friend Sean. Her mistake was asking him about the box."

"His was worse. The longer we thought he was the vic-tim, the more time he had to clear out with the money he'd swindled from his investors. With Jerry Marcus dead, he could start all over again under a new name. Now he's got to use some of that getaway time to stay out of jail."

Karyl's straw gurgled. He set down the glass. "We can't count on him blundering a third time all on his own. He's smart. Crazy-smart: He figured a way around the latest thing in criminal science, and no one else has been able to do that. Beyond that, he doesn't think things through. That's why we need Holly here in town, to force him into making his last mistake."

Our waitress came back, saw that I'd given up on the lamb shank, and asked if I wanted a takeout box.

"No boxes!" I barked.

She paled. I apologized. "Thanks, but I don't think it'll keep. I've still got a lot of running around to do."

She took away my plate. "I hope that means visiting the

Hands-On Museum," Karyl said. "We're proud of it. I'm
tired of giving the same speech every time I see you."

"You've got Marcus wrong. Psychopath, yeah. Mono-
maniac too. He wants to control this case from start to
finish. It isn't about money anymore. Maybe it never was.
People to him are like the ones he makes from scratch
on his computer; they don't whine about motivation or
argue about interpretation or push for percentages of the
gross. He's the kind of movie director who has to call all
the shots."

"He won't call the last. You got Dante Gunnar off the
hook. Take that home."

"You forget I was hired first to find Jerry Marcus."

Our checks came, shattering the chilly silence with a
crack, like ice breaking up. The lieutenant grabbed them
both. "Let the city buy your lunch," he said. "You might
as well get used to it."

I'd thought of asking him if he knew anything about
Alec Moselle. Then I remembered he was a cop, and that
he'd have traced the same number from "Jerry Marcus'"
phone I had, and it would remind him I was still working
an ongoing police investigation. Not that he'd forget; but
there was no percentage in making him any angrier at me
than always.

I walked back to the parking garage and climbed the
stairs to the level where I'd left my car. Another pair of feet
made echoes in the well a flight below, ascending also. I
stopped to light a cigarette. The other footsteps stopped. I
flipped away the match and climbed the rest of the way,
moving at a faster clip. So did the other pair of feet.

The man who belonged to them hovered inside the open door to my level, just inside the shadows. He fumbled at his pockets, looking for those darn keys.

He'd lost them; as I drove past on my way to the street, the screen of a cell phone glowed inside the doorway. I made it to Liberty before I picked up a plain blue Ford in my rearview. There is nothing so well marked as an unmarked police car.

# FIFTEEN

I didn't try to shake loose my shadow. Cops are hard to lose, and after you've gone to all the trouble they just come back angrier. Even when they weren't mad at me I had as much leash as they cared to give me, and not an inch more. I couldn't make a buck without their benediction. They'd find out what I was up to soon enough, tail or no. As it was, the jump I had on them was a rare break.

Anyway, Ann Arbor's not big enough to lose them for long, and they knew the place better than I did.

Driving, I flipped open my notebook and read the address Barry had given me for Alec Moselle, the owner of the last number the dead man in Jerry Marcus' apartment had called. The place was on Washtenaw Avenue. In the downtown Borders I'd picked up a visitor's guide to the city. Jackson Avenue wound eastward past fraternity houses, then metamorphosed into Washtenaw at the foot of a water tower shaped like a bicycle horn with the bulb up top, where the scenery changed from residential to commercial as if someone had flipped a switch. I passed a huge gourmet market and a Barnes & Noble bookstore sharing a jammed parking lot, another Borders, and the usual snarl of sit-down restaurants, coffee shops, takeout joints, coffee shops, auto parts stores, coffee shops, PetSmarts, and two stories of glass with a French name and several yards of neon bent into the shape of a coffee mug leaking scripted steam out the top; I figured none of the natives had slept eight hours straight in years.

The street was multiple lanes of mirror-to-mirror traffic, with just three cars making it through for every green light. I crept along the slow lane, studying the signs in a string of strip malls, spotted the number I was looking for just in time to turn but not in time to signal, and rode the sonic blast from a string of horns into the asphalt lot of a commercial center containing eight businesses separated by common walls on the ground floor and as many on the second. The address I wanted belonged to an outdoor walk-up above a hearing-aid emporium.

I found a diagonal space in front and pretended to be studying my visitor's guide while the anonymous blue Ford drifted past and pulled into a slot between a smoke shop and a place with block M jerseys hanging in its display window. The driver, a clean profile with a flattop haircut, stayed inside while I got out and climbed the metal steps to the second floor. He didn't seem to be taking any precautions to preserve his secret. So far as I could tell he was alone.

An airlock with nothing in it but a linked rubber mat on the linoleum led into a large reception area papered with super-size black-and-white blowup photographs of naked people. Some were artistic studies of lithe young women pouting at something outside the camera's field of vision, others of fat men and white-haired grandmothers, all naked as eggs. The majority were panoramic shots of crowds of men and women of all shapes, ages, and sizes standing on flat roofs and on sidewalks and in parking lots, many of them covering their private parts but just as many putting everything on display, with only the occasional pair of running shoes and caps and scarves with the U of M logo to break up the expanses of skin; these last had all the erotic appeal of a Laundromat. They looked like odes to cellulite.

"Bring along plenty of sunblock," Barry had said. I grinned.

The door behind a doughnut-shaped counter appeared to open by twisting a woman's left nipple. The woman seated inside the doughnut had not posed for the picture. She wore a muumuu printed all over with Route 66 road signs and her hair had been combed into a Woody Woodpecker pompadour only redder, with directional arrows shaved into the temples. She would dress out around three hundred pounds.

"Moze doesn't audition models for the mob shots," she said. "If you'll give me an e-mail address, I'll include you in the next cattle call. All you have to do is show up, and bring along a gym bag or something to put your clothes in when you take them off."

I started to say I wasn't there to audition. Then something beeped and she jerked her head back to look up at me. I saw the headset then, a black band threaded through her topknot with earbuds and a serpent-shaped Madonna transmitter in front of her mouth. She hadn't been talking to me. Like many overweight women she had a pretty, pleasant face, but the expression was stern.

"Moze isn't here, if you're with the police."

"Where is he if I'm not?"

"Are you a reporter? He doesn't give interviews."

I got down to business. The longer I stood there, the further I went down the evolutionary chart; one more bit of idle persiflage and I'd be a U.S. congressman.

"I'm not a reporter. I'm not a cop. I'm not serving papers or unloading *The Watchtower* or collecting signatures for a petition to ban marriages between men and beasts. I'm looking for a missing person. I have reason to believe Mr. Moselle knows him." I gave her a card.

She fished a pair of glasses on a silver chain from the no-man's-land between her breasts and read. "Amos Walker. Ten letters. That's solid. Moze is shooting downtown today."

"A little chilly, isn't it?"

"He works fast. He has to, to avoid arrest. No permit, you know. He always says it's easier to ask forgiveness afterwards than permission before."

"Who does he work for, the American Nudists' Association?"

"He's strictly freelance. Moze celebrates the human body in urban situations." She looked me up and down. "Have you ever considered posing nude?"

"I wear a necktie in the shower."

"You're not wearing a necktie now."

I still had on the black T-shirt and jeans I'd worn to the

Necto Nightclub. They were beginning to feel like a moldy shroud. "I'm in disguise."

"Downtown." She returned my card. "Be prepared to talk on the run. The local authorities differ with him on the definition of art."

"*Where* downtown?"

"You'll know when you're getting close."

I reversed directions, towing my tail. Nearing the central stretch of Main Street the traffic came to a dead halt. Rush hour was still a couple of hours away, but the lights kept changing and nothing moved but hands on horns. I cranked down the window on the passenger's side and hailed a party seated on a bus stop bench under a canopy. He was large and black, wearing a mahogany-colored zoot suit and a sail-brimmed yellow fedora with an orange feather in the band, brown-and-white spectators on his big feet. He had one arm around a guitar case and everything about him glittered, from the heavy gold watch on his wrist to the pearlies in the grin he wore nailed to his face. He was too clean for homeless and dressed too eccentrically for Ann Arbor, where a show handkerchief is looked on as evidence of a narc. I figured I was addressing the town character. When he turned his high beams on me I waved a five-dollar bill.

"They tell me Alec Moselle is shooting someplace around here," I said. "Am I warm?"

"Not if you're posing for Moze." He waved a great dusty-pink palm at the bill. "Keep your money, friend. Might need it if they catch you firing up a doobie. Why you think the place looks like the employee lot at the Ford plant?"

"I've seen more jaywalkers here in the last two days than in thirty years in Detroit. I thought there was a convention in town."

"Follow the crowd, friend."

"How do you suggest I do that?"

He got up for a closer look. The grin glimmered away while he studied my face. After a second he jerked his chin in a nod. "I likes you. Hang on."

Leaving the guitar case on the bench, he stepped into the street, held up one of those flippers, waved his other arm from his hip to his head in a broad arc, and stuck the first one out straight in front of him. Cars started to part, inches at a time, fenders passing close enough to tickle the dust on the ones that needed washing. A horn honked, subtly different from the usual frustrated squawk. Little by little the drivers jockeyed their way between lanes, nosing into the spaces opening up, effectively prying them wider. They flashed their teeth in smiles when they recognized the man directing traffic.

Five minutes after he'd started directing, my lane was open clear to the corner. "What's your name, friend?" I asked as I cruised past the man with the guitar case.

The thousand-candlepower grin came on. "They calls me Shaky Jake, friend. On account of I'm just a bit loose." He pointed a ringed finger at one temple and roared a booming laugh I still hear when things get too quiet.

———

After I turned onto Main Street, I found the crowds on the sidewalks bunched as tightly as the cars on the street. There was no place to park, so I doubled beside a delivery van; it wasn't going anywhere soon. I don't know where the cop tailing me wound up; I'd lost the unmarked car somewhere in the press of metal. The uniformed variety was fanning out to partition off the mob. I guessed they had enough on their hands without dealing tickets. I still had plenty to learn about the city of Ann Arbor.

I bobbed along with the flow toward a Chinese-Japanese restaurant, the kind that features a samurai in a chef's hat juggling razor-sharp knives behind a spitting griddle; that's where the throng had stopped. It was orderly, but the cops forming a human barricade were sweating in fifty-degree temperatures. A red-nosed sergeant and an obvious plain-clothesman stood inside the doorway of a furniture shop, looking as if they didn't know the others. Plainclothes' jaws worked energetically on a wad of gum or a plug of chaw, his fists balled in the pockets of his topcoat.

In front of the restaurant stood an emaciate in army fatigues with a Chicago Bulls cap twisted backward on his head, gesticulating behind a camera on a tripod on a cleared patch of sidewalk while a blonde who looked like Charlize Theron paced back and forth wearing a glisten-ing black all-weather coat. She had that insolent look that's hard to fake when you're wearing something under the coat. And here was one female under thirty who knew how to walk in heels.

So far, Moze—if that was the man in the cap—hadn't overtly broken any laws worth the hassle of embittering a crowd that showed no signs of hostility yet. The humming in the air was electric; the steadily building vibration of waiting. With all the sexual revolutions we've had, the naked operas, NC-17 movies, and grope shows disguised as reality programming, there's nothing like the promise of a naked woman to bring out the herd instinct. The two cops in the doorway watched the woman from under heavy lids, vigilant and patient.

Nothing much happened for sometime. The photographer clacked his shutter, the motor whirred, lining up the next shot of nothing in particular. In sunlight, his fashionable black stubble had bits of red, like pills on a sweater. The crowd began to grumble, the police presence to stiffen further. It looked as if nothing was going to happen; which is the worst thing to happen when enough humanity has gathered in one place expecting Something. It was just the kind of scenario that leads to barn-burning when a lynching falls through. An invisible wire was stretching taut, like one of the strings on Shaky Jake's guitar; if that was what he had in the case. Personally I think it was stuffed with cash.

Then the wire broke.

Moze lifted his cap and resettled it on his head. It might have been a prearranged signal, or maybe his scalp just needed air. His black-red hair ended precisely where the cap began; the rest was pale skin and a splatter of freckles the size of pigeon's eggs.

Signal or not it was enough for the blonde, who twitched loose the belt of her coat, flung off the garment, and struck a Statue of Liberty pose with one arm raised. She was as bare as Venus, without the shell and modest handwork. The camera clacked and whirred against a whoop from the audience.

Things happened fast then. The pair in the doorway boiled out, the red-nosed sergeant swept the coat up from the sidewalk, draping it around her, while the plainclothesman slung up an arm, unconsciously imitating the blonde's gesture. His jaws chomped away at whatever he had between his upper and lower molars.

A prowl car slid growling into the curb. In a flash, the woman was in the backseat and the photographer stood in the middle of the crowd holding a citation. It was as slick a police sweep as I'd ever seen.

The spectators booed and threw plastic cups at the car bearing away their goddess of the afternoon. I went the opposite direction, approaching the man in the Bulls cap.

"Alec Moselle?"

He wasn't paying attention. "I'll be right down with the bail!" he shouted after the car. He looked down at the paper in his hand with a tight smile. It was gone when he looked up at me. "What've *you* got, four nails and a cross?"

"It isn't exactly the Sermon on the Mount, now is it?" I leaned close. There wasn't any need to whisper in that din, but the drama got to me. "Jerry Marcus."

He jerked upright. He was freakishly thin; the bones of his skull were obvious and the fatigues hung on him like something deflated. "Who are you?"

"Does it matter?"

He crumpled the citation into a tight ball and cast it aside. "My trailer." He strode away.

# SIXTEEN

Alec Moselle's trailer was a ten-foot Airstream gleaming like a drop of mercury behind a hulking black Ford F-150 pickup parked at a row of meters. He'd fed them all; he'd risk jail, but not a ticket. Stationary Traffic had the city treed. I hoped they wouldn't tow my car.

It was a truck with character, probably three hundred thousand miles' worth. The front bumper had been replaced with a gray oak four-by-six plank, either because the original had rusted away or he didn't want locked gates getting in the way of a last-minute escape. A female silhouette reclined nude on each back mudflap. The license plate read BARE-S.

"Secretary of State's office wouldn't let me spell it out," he said, shaking loose his keys.

Before I stepped up behind him I swept a glance up and down the street. There was no sign of my piggy-back rider from downtown. Chances are, if he'd lost me in the traffic, he'd cruise around until he spotted the Cutlass and stake it out.

Moselle had gutted the interior and transformed it into a rolling darkroom with an infrared light and damp prints hanging from clothespins like diapers above a stainless-steel sink. Jars of chemicals and boxes of photo paper were stacked on shelves with lips to keep them from spilling over when the trailer turned a sharp corner. Other shelves, canted backward for the same purpose, held coffee table–size photo books with torn jackets: works by Ansel Adams, Margaret Bourke-White, Man Ray, and someone named Bunny Yeager. I asked who she was.

"Fifties pinup queen turned damn good glamour photographer." Moselle leaned his tripod, camera and all, in a corner and deposited a bulky leather-and-canvas camera bag on the table in the dinette. A dwarf refrigerator contained more chemicals and plastic water bottles. He took out two bottles, closed the door with his hip, and offered me one. I took it; I was feeling parched. "I stumbled into my dad's stash of girlie magazines when I was eleven," he said. "Bunny was my first inspiration—as well as the source of a thousand adolescent hard-ons."

On close inspection a print of what I thought were rows of pink baby bottles turned out to be a shot taken from elevation of a crowd of a couple of hundred people in a park setting, all of them naked. The obesity epidemic seemed to have reached crisis proportions.

"That one was a bear." He threw himself into a tattered plaid love seat and pointed his bottle toward a platform rocker listing drunkenly to the left. "The sky was overcast. I had to slow down the shutter and shot six rolls before I got one where nobody moved and blurred the take."

"They were probably shivering. What were you in, a helicopter?"

"A bucket. I borrowed it from a buddy with an Edison crew."

"Any trouble with the law?" I sat in the rocker.

"Not that time. It was a nudist camp on Lake Michigan. Controlled environment. No challenge except from Mother Nature. You can't buy advertising like I got just now."

"Kind of tough on the model."

"I told her what to expect. She was game. She's putting together a portfolio. But you're right. She does all the hard work and gets thrown in the tank. I push a button and get a ticket."

"Which you won't pay."

"I let them pile up, then go in and settle my bill with a brick of cash. That's always good for the front page of the feature section." He tipped up his bottle and let it gurgle for thirty seconds, lowered it, and wiped his lips with the back of a hand. "In this country you can film two guys shooting each other to pieces with Uzis, but the minute they drop their pants you've got a date in court."

"What's the difference between you and a flasher? Remote control?"

"You mean because I keep my clothes on? I helped put myself through college posing for life-drawing classes. Endomorph, you know? Very much in demand." He smacked his nonexistent stomach. "I'm putting together another book: *Ann Arbor Exposed.*"

"You published one before?"

"*The Naked Mile.* Ever hear of it?"

"Sounds like a stretch of unpaved road."

"It was a harmless bit of celebration, but to hear some people talk it was the end of civilization as we know it. Until a few years ago, students at the university had a tradition of streaking starkers across the Diag every spring to mark the end of the semester. It drove the cops and the board of directors apeshit."

"Well, this *is* the cultural center of the world."

"I heard it was the Athens of America." The corners of his mouth twitched. "The adults here are puritans under all that enlightenment crap. They issued statements condemning it, the cops threatened arrests, the *News* editorialized against it—rapists' bait, that old saw. No dice, until the rise of the camera phone and YouTube. Kids who don't mind flopping their privates around in public go all queasy when someone puts them on video. The Naked Mile was gone in a year. But it lives on in my book."

"You shot it?"

"Infrared film at high speed. It was a bitch, and my publishers made me put black bars across their eyes so they couldn't be identified and sue. I don't bother much with releases."

"What was the point?"

He made air quotes with his fingers. "'There are no atheists in foxholes and no hypocrites in the altogether.' I write my own cover copy ever since they tried to sell me as 'Rembrandt in the Raw.'"

I'd known plenty of atheists in Cambodia, but I didn't argue.

"They sold copies in the university bookstore. I was invited to sign. I figured it was a trap, so I turned it down." His lips twitched again. "They call me a pornographer every time I come to town to shoot, but put the stuff between hard covers and suddenly I'm a street artist."

"It's a cockeyed old world." I rocked the chair once, then gave up. It was like hanging off the side of a sloop. "What do you have in common with Jerry Marcus, aside from an interest in photography?"

He sucked on the plastic bottle, caving in the sides and also his cheeks. He was Warsaw Ghetto thin, but he looked healthy. Absent baby fat I put him just past thirty. He shook his head.

"Uh-uh; not yet. You came to me. What about him, aside from the fact I'm not shedding salty tears over his grave? You don't look like a cop."

"Thanks for that." I drank. Introducing water to an empty stomach made me gassy. I tamped down the squirter and set the bottle on the floor. "I'm private, working for a couple he fleeced out of seed money for his film. The number of your studio on Washtenaw came up on Marcus' phone. You were the last person he called."

"That's it?"

I belched, nodded. "I've gotten more from less."

"I'm surprised I haven't heard from the cops."

"You will. Right now they're trying to make the investigation sound like something other than the bottom half of a double bill with *Mr. Alien Elect.*"

When he raised his brows his whole scalp shifted. "Meaning?"

I crossed my legs and sank my hands in my pockets.

"Okay," he said. "Myra put him through. My receptionist. She's new, or she'd have known to tell him I was out on a shoot or dead. I hadn't had a chance to change my number since the last time we spoke."

"Did she say what he wanted?"

"He had an inflated idea of how much money there is in publishing. He tried to tap me for fifty K on that damn space opera. I told him if he called again I'd turn him in to the cops." He crumpled the empty bottle and tossed it at a plastic wastebasket. It circled the rim and came to a stop hanging by the crease, like something by Dali.

"You knew he was running a scam?"

"No, it was something else."

I waited, but he just slung one pipe-cleaner leg over the other and sank his hands in the pockets of his duffel jacket.

I said, "Marcus only skinned my clients out of fifteen. At the rate he was going, he stood to clear his first million before he finished one reel. I'm surprised he shot as much as he did."

"Oh, he was serious about it when we were partners."

"You were partners?"

"Three years ago. I co-wrote the script, about invading aliens who combust simultaneously when cornered. We were shooting digitally and computer-generating the special effects.

"We had the same brainstorm at the same time," he said, becoming animated. "If you can fake an organic explosion, why not fake the organism? He was years ahead of the bulge in Hollywood when it came to simulation. He found a way to make the characters look like real people instead of inflated dolls. I told him he should hire himself out, but he said he couldn't work for anyone else. I don't understand how he did what he did, but I'm a still photog. I prefer working the old-fashioned way, with film and older processes. Back at the studio I've got equipment designed by Louis Daguerre. It was fun, though, making movies; or it was until he changed."

"You mean turned crooked."

"Not crooked. Not then. Shit." He twirled a finger next to his temple, reminding me of Shaky Jake. "He rewrote the ending to herd the aliens into the Michigan Theater and send them up like Roman candles, and the building with them. Make *Independence Day* look like a Looney Tune."

"Exciting."

"More exciting than my heart could take," he said. "He wasn't planning to do it on the computer."

# SEVENTEEN

Cars swished by outside. The traffic jam he'd created was breaking up, with or without the assistance of the big man in the mahogany-colored suit. I said nothing while Moze plunked the heels of his combat boots onto a low table littered with aluminum film canisters and curling Polaroids of uninterrupted flesh. He folded his hands behind his head. The cords in his neck stood out like umbrella staves.

"Jerry made a student film when he was studying at the U of M, entered it in competition at the Cinema Slam. Know what that is?"

"Sounds like a stretch of unpaved road." I plugged my grin with a cigarette.

"Go ahead and light up if you want to see the moon before you die. Just give me two blocks' head start." He patted a floor cabinet. "It took a permit to transport some of these chemicals. Can't fight the AAPD *and* ATF."

I put it back in the pack.

"It's an amateur film festival," he said. "The entrants screen their masterpieces for the public at the Michigan Theater during the art fairs. All the Spielberg wannabes try to turn them into a gig in Hollywood, or at least a grant from the National Endowment for the Arts. The audiences get in for free and watch the films, eat bratwurst, drink beer, and fill out critique cards to be mailed to the film-makers later."

"How'd Marcus do, as if I couldn't guess?"

"They were less than impressed."

"Was it the sci-fi?"

"No, it was one of those allegorical pieces of tripe you hear students read out loud in creative writing courses the world over, only with shaky-cams and long lingering close-ups at the end of the scene so you know it's Signifi-cant, with a capital *S*. Symbolism by the long ton. It was technically sound—he was a world-beater there—but naïve to the point of pain. Some people liked it. Most thought it was pretentious and boring."

"I take it he didn't react well to criticism."

"I didn't know him yet then; he shot the film when he was a sophomore. I only saw it when he showed it to me our senior year. But he couldn't stop talking about that night. He never forgave Ann Arbor."

"Still, it's a big jump from there to blowing up a theater."

"The Michigan isn't just another theater. It's one of those grand motion-picture palaces from the twenties. It lan-guished for years—at one point the owners painted over all the fretwork and gold leaf in university maize-and-blue—and then it was going to be pulled down and turned into a parking lot. They love parking lots here the way Detroit loves crack houses; you can park in one to visit another. Then a group of preservationists took up a collection and bought the building and got the city to invest in restoring it. You have to see it before you go home: It's like they hung the Hanging Gardens of Babylon inside the Taj Mahal and shoved it up the ass of the Colossus of Rhodes."

"You paint a pretty picture, but I don't know if I'll find the time."

"Your loss. It's a local institution, like Zingerman's and stoplights. By destroying it, Jerry would be getting back at the Slam and the community both at once. I think by the time we split he'd forgotten the whole thing started out as a movie production."

"He said that, about getting back?"

"He showed me. You know Whitmore Lake? Don't say it sounds like a stretch of unpaved road."

"I know it. I helped enroll a couple of juvies in the reform school there."

"Nice little town, if you like ice cream cones in the summer and freezing your ass off pulling pike out from under the ice in winter. I like Edy's and Mrs. Paul's. He took me out to a storage shed there, which he had stacked to the rafters with a couple of hundred bags of fertilizer. He wasn't planning on going into farming."

I nodded. It was the same volatile ingredient used in the Oklahoma City bombing.

"He said he'd spent six months putting it together,

buying two and three bags at a time from places all over southeastern Michigan and northern Ohio. Buy too much in one place and you'll find ATF agents camping on your doorstep when you get home."

"A lot of people died in Oak City," I said. "Was he talking about blowing up just a piece of architecture?"

"He said. But the theater's on Liberty, in one of the biggest commercial districts in the city and just off campus. You'd have to evacuate it for five blocks in every direction."

I wanted a cigarette, but I didn't care to see the moon that season. I wanted to rock, but I felt queasy enough just from the conversation. "He knew how to make a bomb?"

"He studied demolition. In Hollywood you have to be a certified explosives expert to work in special effects: squibs and things, so it looks like an actor got shot to pieces instead of just getting ketchup stains all over his costume. That's before he found out he was a genius and that geniuses don't work for wages. Pauline Kael's book on *Citizen Kane* changed his life."

I hadn't seen a copy in Marcus' room. I wondered if that was significant.

"So he showed you the fertilizer, and that's when you broke away."

He got up all of a piece, like a Swiss Army knife folding itself, and paced the length of the trailer. It shifted on its springs.

"If I had, I'd have tipped off the authorities first. I didn't really think he'd go through with it. Acting out his fantasy as far as he had was as good as the real thing, I thought.

You'd have to have known Jerry. I doubt he ever went so far as to bait a mousetrap, knowing what would happen to the mouse."

"Not to mention what would happen to the guy who helped bait it."

He stopped pacing, glared down at me. His eyes rolled like marbles in those naked sockets. "If I thought I might be implicated in a real atrocity, don't you think I'd have run, not walked, to the nearest police station?"

"Before today, I never thought I'd meet a man who took pictures of mobs in the altogether and sold it as art. I don't know you, Moselle."

"Sure." He slung himself back onto the love seat. The bill of his cap got in the way when he tilted his head against the cushions. He tore it off and flung it at the wastebasket. This time he scored. "Anyway, he gave up the idea after September eleventh. Those high-flying bastards spooked him sane. I helped him truck the bags of animal shit out into the country and dumped 'em in a swamp. It must be pretty green there by now."

"What swamp? Someone may want to check."

"How the hell should I know? I was brought up in Chicago. He rented a U-Haul and did the driving—he could hardly have fitted that load in that circus-wagon Mustang of his—and it was dark. By the time we finished dumping it I was soaked through with sweat and slime and cowshit; the fucking bags leaked. Next morning I felt like I'd been rolled by a pack of gorillas; I'd've needed a crane to pull my pants on, so I spent the day in bed. It was enough to make me look for another line of work where my training would pay off; not movies, and not for chrissake unloading offal into Okefenokee."

He scratched his bald head. It was so pale between freckles his nails left pink marks.

"Frankly, I was happy when he decided to swap terrorism for fraud. Even serial killers seem warm and fuzzy after those guys."

"Marcus skews smart," I said after a moment.

"That's an understatement. He scored fifteen-fifty on his SATs. Next to him, Ted Kaczynski is Forrest Gump."

"I don't mean that. I mean he read your reaction to his plan and decided it was worth going to all that trouble to convince you he'd abandoned it."

He stopped scratching. "You got that from what?"

"Dead reckoning. Anyone who can fake his own murder by salting the corpse with his own DNA can drag a dead skunk across his path well enough to throw off the one man who could stop him from collecting on the debt he thinks he's owed."

"One of my bottles must've sprung a leak. Either that, or you were drunk when you came in here. What do you mean about faking his murder? Jerry's dead. I knew him better than anyone. You think I wouldn't know if he were still alive?"

"ESP." I yawned; not for effect. I hadn't spent so many hours awake since the Tet Offensive. "Stands for Every Silly Presumption. He's as alive as that future *Sports Illustrated* model you just sent to the clink. Where were you a week ago Saturday?"

He smiled full out; I realized then why he'd resisted before. He looked like the label on a bottle of poison.

"Cheering for the enemy. I was at Northwestern two years before I met Jerry. It's the only game I ever attend. I was there all afternoon, with friends. They'll remember, because I was lucky not to get the crap beaten out of me for calling the home team Nectarines. You can ask them right now, if you like." He excavated a cell from a cargo pocket.

"No point. If you were guilty they'd be coached. Anyway, if your only beef was with Jerry Marcus, I'd have to go back to square one for a motive. He's alive."

The smile set in concrete. "You said that before. Sell me."

"I don't have the training. You'll have to go to the boys and girls in ice-cream jackets for that. Jerry Marcus isn't dead. The cops think he's the murderer, not the victim."

He sprang to his feet again, like a drawerful of scissors; clawed open the refrigerator, mangled the cap off another bottle of water, and drained it in one draft. The look on his narrow face said he wished it were something else.

# EIGHTEEN

mpossible."

He was pacing again. The trailer felt like a tugboat entering the English Channel.

"That's what the cops say," I said. "I haven't heard from the white coats, but I doubt you could quote them in a family newspaper."

"No one can manufacture DNA, not even Jerry. I know you can't just mix it up in a test tube and inject it into a corpse and expect the police to think it's you lying there, and I flunked science."

"Hey, me, too. Should we start a club?"

He stopped, his head bowed to keep from colliding with the curved ceiling. "Does murder always tickle you like this?"

"Depends on the murder. For the record, I'm with Lieutenant Karyl. Fingerprints have been around long enough to stand the test of time. Even then I'm not convinced that no two sets are alike until they print the entire population in the history of the world. I saw a snowflake last January that looked exactly like one I saw in 'seventy-eight."

"So who's dead, if it isn't Jerry?"

"We'll ask him when we find him."

"That's police work."

"They're shorthanded. I help out where I can."

"You wouldn't be sweet on this Holly character, by any chance?"

"Too young. I'd have to explain too much to her just to have an argument. I hired on to find Jerry Marcus. I don't know why I have to keep reminding people of that."

"I guess you don't have to take your pants off after all to prove you're not a hypocrite."

"Thanks, though I am proud of my legs."

He looked at a watch strapped to the underside of his wrist. "Shit. I've got to bail out my model. All she's got on is a raincoat."

I put a card on the low table, stood my water bottle on top of it, and got up. "Call me if you hear from Marcus."

"I won't hear from him. After I turned him down, he topped off his getaway stake somewhere else. Otherwise he wouldn't have gone ahead with the murder. He wasn't—isn't—the impulsive type. Damn. Now I have to change my tenses all over again."

"You better hope you're right. If what you said about blowing up the Michigan Theater wasn't just a fantasy, you're one of two witnesses who can tie him to a major crime—conspiracy, in your case. Sooner or later he's got to remember you might throw him to the wolves to save your own skin. He's a murderer now. He's got nothing to lose by finishing what he started."

Moze fished his cap from the wastebasket and put it on, this time with the bill in front. He swept a long skinny arm around his portable developing lab. "I'm safe as houses. You might have noticed I attract crowds wherever I go."

"Crowds don't scare him. He made his last move on a well-lit street just as the bars were emptying out." I opened the door. "You wouldn't have that model's phone number, by any chance?"

"Waste of time. She's engaged to the coach of a girls' high school swim team."

A tall female cop and a squat party in putty-colored coveralls carrying the logo of the delivery van I'd double-parked next to were standing on the sidewalk, waiting for the tow truck. The plainclothesman who'd been following me all over town had pulled his blue Ford into a loading zone to watch. I waited until the pair on the sidewalk were looking another direction, then slid under the wheel and drove away from the shouting with a fresh ticket flapping from under one of my wipers. The Ford chirped rubber catching up.

At a stoplight I put the Cutlass in park, got out, and walked back to the unmarked car, making a twirling motion with one hand. The window whirred down on the driver's side. He was an ex-Marine type, jarhead and all, with a tiny silver crucifix glittering on a thin chain around a neck as big around as a leg of lamb. The hand not resting on the wheel hovered near the lapel of his windowpane-plaid sportcoat.

"I'm going home to snooze," I said. "Home being Detroit. You might be late for supper."

His lower teeth showed in a piranha smile. "No problem, Mac. My wife left me for a CSI."

I drove all the way back to Detroit with the cop trailing behind like the tail of a kite. I kept below the speed limit; the signs were blurring and shadows stood out from the pavement in 3-D effect, an optical illusion. My eyes scratched in their sockets. I felt like old copper extruded past its limit.

The house had a lonely feel, as if a large boisterous family had moved out ten years ago. I walked from room to room, swinging my arms and bellowing yawns. I was more tired than I was hungry, and I was as hungry as a rabbi marooned in a Bob Evans. But before I turned in I called Holly Zacharias.

"Dad's gonna be pissed," she said. "I don't think he can get his money back on that plane ticket."

"I'm glad the cops caught up with you before you gave up on me and called for a taxi. How many officers did they put on you?"

"Two in a car under my window. I'm not sure about the dude sitting at the bus stop. He's let two buses go past, but he could be OCD."

"Keep your cell handy whenever you go out, okay? Having it out in the open can ward off trouble."

"You really think I'm still in danger? 'In danger,' God!

I sound like one of those wussy teenagers in a slasher movie."

"The more I find out about Marcus the worse he looks. Keep in sight of your escort, and stay off the front porch."

"Sean's gonna think I threw him over for a couple of pigs."

I didn't think that was such a bad trade, but I didn't say so. I told her I'd see what I could do about that plane ticket. I didn't say what. You never know who's listening.

I undressed completely and was asleep the second I drew the covers up to my chin. I dreamed I was running through a crowd of naked people who kept bursting into flame.

When I woke up it was light out. That was a surprise, because I felt as rested as if I'd been asleep for hours. I solved the mystery when I looked out the window and saw the sun was in the east toward Windsor. I'd been out halfway around the clock.

My belly button was scraping my spine; at last I knew what "peckish" meant. I found two cans of sardines in a cupboard, polished them off standing at the sink, and chased them with a quart of milk. Afterward I was still hungry, but less likely to take a bite out of the cop I knew was still waiting for me outside, unless someone had spelled him. I showered, shaved, and put on a suit. The man in the mirror looked like a defendant dressed by his lawyer to fool a jury. After the T-shirt, the necktie was like a choke collar, but at least I felt clean.

The commute had gotten to be a drag. I packed an overnight bag, put it in the car by way of the door from the kitchen, and then went out the front.

The vet in the blue Ford sat up straight. He looked alert, if rumpled. I hoped a night's sleep in the car hadn't wrecked his back. Our friendship was long-standing. I whistled at him and pointed at the garage. He nodded and started his motor. I swung up the door, drove out the Cutlass, went back to pull the door shut, and snatched the ticket from the windshield before getting back in. If I didn't start paying them soon I'd have to buy a car with a bigger glove compartment.

We headed west. The Athens of America it wasn't, but Ann Arbor had me by the short hairs.

Back on East Liberty, I passed the Michigan Theater. This time I paid closer attention to the Romanesque façade. It looked like a cathedral in some small Italian village owned by the Church. A Chinese film was playing that day, judging by the unfamiliar names of the actors. The electric bulbs chased the title around the towering marquee. It was a commercial feature aimed at the art-house circuit, but the visitor's guide had confirmed what Alec Moselle had told me about the Cinema Slam: For a few days each July, amateur movie critics could go in and watch the seminal work of fledgling filmmakers like Jerry Marcus and weigh in. They'd weighed in on Jerry, soundly enough to sour him on the city. He'd fantasized about destroying the theater, even taken steps to do it, then had fallen back on the relatively mild alternative of separating local investors from their money; *then* faked his own murder, using a real corpse.

So it had been a full week for him, and it wasn't over yet. Trying to predict the next move of a certified lunatic is like boxing someone else's shadow.

Whatever he did next, it wouldn't involve Holly Zacharias. I don't promise myself much, but I was going to hold myself to that, with or without the cooperation of law enforcement. To do that I needed the devil's own plan. Fortunately, I had just the devil in mind.

# PART THREE

# LOOP

# NINETEEN

'd trade the inconvenience of not owning a portable phone for the luxury of placing a call from the interior of a vintage booth in the Michigan Union. It's gone now, along with the others, with no plaque in their place to commemorate the fact that they ever existed. It was perfumed with oak, tung oil, and the ghosts of generations of good cigars, and the horsehide upholstery stuffed with down was like wearing a heat wrap around my back; all those trips between Detroit and Ann Arbor had my lumbar region shooting out little bolts of lightning like in a comic strip. The cozy little cells were too good to withstand the twenty-first century.

Barry's cell wasn't answering. I tried his landline at home. He picked up after three rings.

"I hope they're paying you in quarters," he said when I told him who was calling.

"I just bought two rolls. This is going to take a lot longer than three minutes."

"I never get tired of asking if there's anything for me."

"Everything, if you'll sit on it till I say; and do me one more little favor."

"Call me back and reverse the charges. The little guy with a pitchfork on my left shoulder tells me I can deduct them next April."

I hung up and got the operator. At the end of a quarter of an hour, during which I told him what I'd gotten from Alec Moselle, I spent one of my coins on a much shorter conversation with Holly Zacharias.

The university tower was caroling four o'clock when she came my way across the Diag, carrying a camo duffel slung from its strap on one shoulder. She wore the student uniform: tank top, bell-bottoms, and sandals. Her hair hadn't grown out any, but something was missing. I figured it out while I was throwing the duffel in the backseat.

"You took the hardware out of your face."

"I didn't want to set off the metal detectors."

"You look fourteen years old."

"Thanks. Like I don't get carded enough."

"Same flight as yesterday?"

"Yeah. Dad lucked out. The exchange only cost him twenty bucks extra. He bitched about it five minutes. He's an okay dad, just cheap."

"He's going to bitch some more."

"What?"

"On the way. Any extra baggage?"

"No, just the—oh, you mean cops. I don't think so. I

went into the parking garage on Thompson and ducked out the other side. I guess nobody told them I don't have a car."

"It's okay. I brought along reinforcements." I jerked my thumb back over my shoulder at the faithful blue Ford. "He's got a crush on me. I think it's my aftershave."

She glanced at Captain America behind the wheel, shook her head. "Just when I think I got you old dudes figured out, you throw me a curve."

"We get old for reasons. Buckle up. We're in for a bumpy ride."

"Where do I think I heard that before?"

"The Michigan Theater, probably. Sooner or later they had to have got around to Bette Davis." I let out the clutch, throwing her back into the seat. Every once in a while it's reassuring to impress youth with a virile show.

We drove down State Street. The blue Ford closed within a length. The point of the tail was to keep me from smuggling my passenger out of town, and my direction had Sergeant York upright with both fists on the wheel.

I lit a cigarette, flipped the match into the slipstream, and offered her the pack.

She shook her head.

"I don't really smoke. I only do it sometimes to make people disapprove. I don't guess you know why that's important."

"It isn't. But it beats Sodoku."

"Where are we going?"

I'd turned south on Main Street. "Airport. You have a flight at six."

"Double back and take I-94. US-23's under construction near the interchange."

"I know. I like to watch my tax dollars at work. A road crew in my block spent a month filling a pothole the size of a cereal bowl."

"If it's backed up I'll miss my plane."

"You're going to miss it anyway."

She turned my way. Her window was open. The wind stirred the stubble on her scalp. "My dad'll shit if I don't show up on time at O'Hare."

"Does anyone show up on time at O'Hare?"

She glanced back over her shoulder. "This have anything to do with the blockhead in the Ford?"

"This has everything to do with the blockhead in the Ford. For the record, he isn't a blockhead. I tried everything to expose him for one and he didn't rise. He's just a guy doing his job."

"Stake me out like a goat. Cops," she spat.

"They've got bills to pay, same as everyone else." I tipped the butt out the window. It was like sucking on a lump of coal. "Zacharias. That's Greek, right? Studying ancient civilizations?"

"Minoring in Poli Sci," she said. "So the answer's yeah."

"Going to run for office? I mean after you turn loose Moby Dick?"

"Shamu. Gonna nail the ones that run. TV reporter."

"Taking journalism?"

"Just one course. I dropped out when the instructor said the business of a newspaper is to make money."

I laughed.

She swung back my way. "I said something funny?"

"Yeah, but that wasn't why I laughed. When I was six, I asked my mother what my father did for a living. She said, 'He makes money.' So that's what I thought he did, printing bills on a press."

She faced front. "I wish I knew what you were talking about half the time."

"I'm an enigma," I said, "wrapped in a mystery, with a chewy caramel center."

"Shi-i-it!" She laughed then.

Orange barrels ganged up on us near the I-94 interchange. I got out of that lane. So did the blue Ford. I accelerated and changed again, passing traffic on the right. The Ford changed too. With the barricade coming up I closed in again on the outside lane. A green Corvette sped up to shut me out, braked when our fenders kissed: Steel trumps fiberglass. Brakes screeched behind. I got into the space and stopped to avoid rear-ending a truck. I still hear the screech late at night. The green Corvette's horn blasted. The blue Ford halted short of the barricade.

My pet cop was still waiting for a break when the pace began to pick up. When a semi in the other lane lagged back to downshift I used the square inch of space and pushed the pedal to the floor. The four-barrel carburetor kicked in with an atomic blast. We hit ninety with a whump. I rolled up my window against the booming wind. Holly did the same, and we were sealed in silence with a gray blur on either side. There was no sign of the Ford when I made the interchange, floating on air two inches under both right tires. My knuckles swelled white on the wheel.

I braked, slewing onto the shoulder and spraying gravel. As we powered down, Holly pried her fingers from the dash. "Where'd you learn to drive?" It came from two inches below her larynx.

"The Phnom Penh highway. It's less interesting without land mines." I leveled off at seventy, with cars passing me. It felt like I could open the door and step out for air. "He'll go on to the airport and look for us there."

"I think I'll take that cigarette now."

I lit one off the dash lighter and handed it over. She took two shallow puffs, opened her window a crack, let it free, and sucked in air from outside. "Where to now?"

"Rest stop."

"I don't have to."

"Me neither."

I turned off into a roadside oasis with a faux-fieldstone building advertising toilets, refreshments, and tourist brochures. Barry Stackpole was waiting for us in the parking lot, leaning on a yellow Land Rover with black trim, like a flashlight. He was my age, but looked as if he'd been packed away in dry ice after extra work in *Rebel Without a Cause*. In those days he still camouflaged his missing fingers in a flesh-colored cotton glove. The artificial leg and aluminum patch on his scalp concealed more subtly.

"Nice ride." I shook his good hand. "What's rhinoceros taste like?"

"It's a loaner. I got a Central American drug dealer off Death Row. Good family man, loves his kids. He's letting me use it while he serves three consecutive life sentences in Huntsville. Uses more fuel than the *Exxon Valdez*." He smiled at Holly. "Anyone ever tell you you look like Jamie Lee Curtis?"

"I thought the same thing," I said.

"Tony Curtis' daughter." She smiled at my reaction. "I saw *True Lies,* and I've got Turner Classic Movies on a pirate hook-up. *The Black Shield of Falworth* rocks."

"Barry Stackpole, Holly Zacharias," I said. "Proper introductions later. Get in." I swung open the door on the passenger's side of the Land Rover.

She climbed up onto the seat. I put her duffel in the back, gave Barry an envelope with train fare and the clipping with Jerry Marcus' picture. "Michigan Central Station. If you see him, holler for security."

"Too slow." He made his youthful face and showed me a walnut handle in an underarm clip. I hadn't known he owned a firearm.

Holly said, "Hey."

I smiled at her. "Tell your dad he can bill me for the airline ticket. I'll charge it to expenses."

She shook her head. Without a face full of metal she had a brilliant smile. "You represent—for a Boomer dude."

I waved as they pulled away. Her I'd miss. She was better company when she wasn't trying to make people disapprove of her.

# TWENTY

I was a fugitive, but only so long as it took Lieutenant Karyl's detail to find out I hadn't taken Holly Zacharias to the airport, check back with Ann Arbor, and track me down at my office in Detroit or my house outside Hamtramck.

That wouldn't take long; he'd have followed up on us both the moment the officers he'd put on Holly reported she'd given them the slip. I wouldn't have wanted to be on their end of that conversation; when a callow coed outsmarts months of training and years of experience, all his Hungarian ancestry would come out, going back to Vlad the Impaler.

Better he burn himself out on them than on me. I'd committed one felony, possibly more, and made a significant contribution to road rage, Michigan's chief export and a commodity that is never in short supply.

I drove home with one eye on the speedometer and the other on the rearview mirror, looking for prowl cars and unmarked blue Fords. Those twelve unconscious hours came in handy, also the inadequacy of my breakfast. The sardines and milk were long digested, leaving the blood flow entirely to the brain, where I most needed it.

Nevertheless I exited at the first sign of a pair of golden arches and dropped blazing hot coffee on top of a double cheeseburger. While I was waiting for my order, a siren yelped in the same block. When I climbed back down from the headliner, the kid at the window shook his head. "Happens all the time; except last month, when somebody stuck up the place. Took 'em twenty minutes to get here, and the station's just around the corner." He grinned. "Bet if we was a Dunkin' Donuts—"

I snatched the sack and cup out of his hands and drove off.

At the restaurant exit I passed a couple of opportunities to turn into the street while a set of flashing red-and-blue lights swung onto the ramp of the expressway a block and a half beyond. A polite tap on a horn behind me sent me on my way.

In a situation like that it sometimes helps to remind oneself of one's pressing responsibilities. Staying out of jail topped the list. But then it did so often it had become almost an abstract concept, like breathing and smoking tobacco.

Drawing a murderer's attention from Holly, an eyewitness who could put Jerry Marcus in state housing for life, came next. It meant setting myself up as a decoy; he had to shift his concentration to me, strong enough to rearrange his own priorities.

That meant finding him first, which was the job I'd hired on for at the beginning, back when it was a simple case of possible fraud.

There were so many things wrong with that it made me tired all over again. I tossed the cheeseburger half-eaten back into the sack and deep-broiled my tongue with nuclear-grade coffee. Something was wrong with it. I looked at the plastic lid. The little blister they push in with a thumb to identify the contents told me I was drinking decaf.

I woke up from a beautiful dream, where it was always summer, with fireflies blinking on and off like tiny neon lights and brooks jabbering like old men on a park bench and my parents alive and in good health—and tore the steering wheel left, away from the rumble strips leading to a bridge abutment. A helpful truck driver whomped his air horn at me as he swept past, walloping the Cutlass in his wake. You can't store up sleep. Wherever they keep the account books, some bean counter is measuring half a day's rest against thirty-four hours awake and recording it in red ink.

I needed to get wheels out from under me, if only for a couple of hours. Michigan Avenue was coming up. It's the main drag through Ypsilanti, a community built on the World War II Willow Run Ford aircraft plant, since grafted on to Ann Arbor to the west with no seams in between: Some still call it Ypsi-tucky, after the Southerners who'd swarmed up US-23 to work for top wages building B-25 bombers.

I passed up a Holiday Inn, a Ramada, and a Comfort

Suites as too accessible to a preliminary investigation. In an open area just past a truss barn called the Da-Glo Massage, with fraternity insignia plastered on the glass front door, I pulled around behind two stories of Korean War construction called the Wagon Wheel Motel. A pair of whitewashed tires flanked the driveway, half-sunk in concrete. They hadn't even bothered to score real wagon wheels. I wondered how Michelin had managed to miss the place.

There was a package-liquor store across the alley; there would be. I dumped the disposable cup still steaming in a bullet-shaped trash can by the store entrance and commissioned a fifth of Old Smuggler from the unsmiling Arab behind the counter. They throw them in with the fixtures.

I entered the hotel through a side door and followed a dim prefab hallway to a foyer adjacent to a gaggle of tables and chairs and a stainless-steel serve-yourself counter. It was deserted in late afternoon except for a lazy fly practicing its stalls under the glass cover of a warming tray.

A clerk who waxed his handlebars extolled the virtues of the free continental breakfast from behind the registration desk, but all I heard was directions to the elevators. His moustache didn't twitch when I paid cash, but he did look to see I had bags; the fact that one was a paper sack meant as much to him as Austrian edelweiss. The halls smelled of disinfectant with a spearmint base.

"Smoking or non?" he'd asked.

"Smoking."

He glanced at an electric clock. "We've got just the one. It isn't ready yet."

I looked at the clock: 6:22. "When's checkout?"

"Eleven; but the housekeeper had trouble rousing the guest. The young lady he checked in with—" He moved a shoulder. We were men of the world. I must have looked even more worn-out than I felt.

"Yeah. I don't know why they bother to steal the pants when the wallet's all they want."

He looked pained; and I look like Brad Pitt. "If you want to go out for a bite while you're waiting, I can recommend—"

I'd seen all the restaurants within walking distance: Aunt Emma's, The Chicken Palace, Steaks-'n'-More, an all-you-can-eat buffet without a single car in its parking lot. Steaks-'n'-More had a fiberglass cow on its flat roof, so the filet would be from Secretariat out of Dream Queen. The chain places were just the same thing with a national advertising campaign.

"What've you got in nonsmoking?"

He slid a key card through his thingamajig and presented it with a flourish. "Two twenty-six. Second floor."

The ice machine made a noise like a Cape buffalo hacking up a tourist and spat three cubes into the plastic bucket I got from the clerk. I left them there, bucket and all, and carried my bottle with me into the room.

It was long and narrow, with blackout curtains that drenched it in early Castle Dracula. I switched on the overhead light, inspected the bathroom for bushwhackers: a couple of cracked tiles, rust stains in the tub, a water bug the size of a grape clinging insolently to the wall above the mirror, which had been wiped down with an oil rag. There was a chute next to the light switch for disposing the kind of razor blades they haven't made since *Dragnet.*

Everything straight out of the catalogue: *Nihilism for Dummies.*

The TV, at least, was a modern flat-screen, but the remote didn't work. Fourteen typewritten pages in a loose-leaf notebook encouraged me to slide a credit card into the phone and watch Midnight Cinema twenty-four/seven. *Prongs of New York* caught my eye.

The window looked out on the parking lot, and a rail-thin party in a hoodie peering through car windows looking for keys left in the ignition. He slouched past my car without pausing. I keep it battered and unwashed for a reason.

The lock on the window was broken. I'd have been disappointed otherwise. I laid the remainder of my store of quarters in the track so it couldn't slide open any more than to admit a man's head, unless he put some shoulder into it. I unshipped the Chief's Special from my belt clip and laid it on the nightstand on the side of the bed opposite the window, massaged the dent it had made next to my kidney.

I'd spent my life in that room; the place might have belonged to a chain, each one sprung up simultaneously, unaware of all the others, like toadstools exposed to the same conditions. You know them by their shared features: The radiator/air conditioner under the windows that blasts sopping heat in July, Little America cold in January; the toilet that runs like Pimlico and the sink that drains like the Colorado River carving the Grand Canyon, centimeter by centimeter, eons at a time; the damp spot in the carpet that never dries; the plastic fingernail on the floor behind the headboard, five years out of fashion; the fat phone book that opens automatically to the section on escort agencies ("Discreet Services—Charge Shows up as Entertainment"); the remote you handle with a wad of tissues if you handle it at all—if the tissues in the dispenser have been replaced; three squares of toilet paper left on the roll; the maids who bang on your door at 7:00 A.M., and when you're gone for the day never come in to clean and change the towels; Handi Wipes pretending to be washcloths; that self-righteous little tent on the bed asking you to throw any linen you want changed on the floor, otherwise Let's Protect Our Precious Water Supply (and also our city bill); the double lock that makes a satisfying clunk when you turn it, but when you tug on the knob the door opens without resistance, halted only by a thin metal chain designed for a charm bracelet; the wake-up call that never comes, unless it comes two hours early; the little pack of five-dollar cashews in the minibar; the forty-watt bulb over the mirror in the bathroom; the shower that goes from lukewarm to scalding in half a second, and a half-second later to icicles. The Gideon Bible in the nightstand drawer, stuck fast to whatever someone had spilled inside while watching *Seinfeld*. The call to the front desk that rings and rings and rings. The wag who sets the electric alarm clock for 3:00 A.M. just before he checks out, as a raspberry to the stranger who succeeds him. And all night long, adolescent feet pounding the hallway outside in their size fourteen Crocs.

All to be expected, although not always all at once. That kind of dead-solid consistency belongs only to the inevitable sibilant sound of the bill sliding under the door at four in the morning, marked up 50 percent to address taxes.

A bulb in one of the lamps was burned out. The air in the nonsmoking room smelled of stale Chesterfields. I dismantled the smoke detector attached to the ceiling, but I needn't have bothered; the batteries were caked with green mold. I hung my jacket and tie in the open closet, kicked off my shoes, joined the bedbugs on the slick green coverlet, lit up, and blew a cloud of smoke toward a ceiling stained gold with nicotine. I broke the seal on the bottle and took a swig of putative Scotch. It tasted like gym socks put up in heather.

I had to laugh then. It was just the kind of place Mrs. Stevens had warned me I'd wind up in if I didn't play well with the other children in third grade.

# TWENTY-ONE

Old motels are excellent conductors of sound. A TV murmured in an adjoining room, toilets flushed, a shower whooshed, whistled, and shut off with a thump. An alarm clock buzzed and kept buzzing for five minutes. A wing of the place was reserved for extended-stay guests; this one was a nightwatchman or a jazz musician or worked the graveyard shift at a plant, and he slept as hard as a bear in January. I anesthetized myself with a second glass and drifted off, but liquor has a backlash effect, snapping you into full wakefulness an hour or two after you pass out. I got up, cleared the coins out of the track, opened the window, and stood there smoking. Nothing doing down in the parking lot: no shadowy figures smoking cigarettes in doorways, not even a muttering old dog lifting its leg against a lamppost. But always the hum of tires on Washtenaw Avenue and on the US-23/I-94 interchange. If you closed your eyes and used your imagination it might have been the surf off Maui; but only if the heater worked.

It was a time for quiet reflection, of taking stock of one's choices, past and present; but all I saw was my own tired reflection in the glass, and my portfolio was empty. I ditched the butt, put the window back together, and went back to bed.


The same construction crew that had been working on every motel I'd ever checked into was up at dawn, pneumatic hammers whirring and thudding, roto-mills chewing up asphalt, power saws wailing like Godzilla on the pot. I stood under needle spray for ten minutes, scraped my chin, put on the same suit but fresh everything else, and went down to savor the pleasures of the continental breakfast.

The same fly was drifting around inside the glass cover, browsing this time among a pile of bagels that looked hard enough to bust a window. There was the usual mess of scrambled eggs, runny as a rain gutter, bruised bananas, individual-size boxes of Sugar Frosted Diabetes, and not enough flatware. I decided the coffee wouldn't kill me, but the yellow stuff that trickled out of the spigot argued the point. I dumped it, cup and all, in the trash can and went to the desk in the lobby.

A different clerk, this one a short blonde, was at her computer. They used to be all the time sorting mail; now their eyes are pasted to an Etch A Sketch. She asked if I'd enjoyed my stay.

"You forgot my spa appointment."

"I'm sorry?"

"It was fine. You need to replace one of the lightbulbs."

After I left, I felt ashamed of myself for the spa remark. I'd stayed worse places.

A chicken wearing a chef's hat on the sign of the restaurant next door advertised family dining. Inside the converted double-wide house trailer I sat at a laminated table near the windows and ordered steak and eggs and coffee. A white-haired couple at the next table discussed storm windows the whole time I waited.

The waitress brought back a shoe heel and a single fried egg; but the coffee turned my electrolytes back on.

A six-year-old boy dressed like Dennis the Menace— striped shirt, overalls, the works—toddled my way and stood watching me eat. I was getting a lot of that lately; I must look like someone's grandfather.

I glanced around for the boy's parents, but the only likely candidate, a thirtyish woman reading the classifieds in the *Observer,* wasn't paying attention. I smiled at the kid and asked if he was going to grow up to be a cowboy.

That ended his interest in me. He toddled off straight to Mr. and Mrs. Storm Windows and climbed onto a chair. I wondered, not for the first time, if I was in the wrong line of work.

Passing the crew in the motel parking lot, I kept alert. Nobody ducked in and out of hedges, no helicopters buzzed me. I wasn't worth the fuel.

But I was worth something.

An Ypsilanti cruiser passed me going the other direction on Washtenaw, slowed as it drew abreast of the Cutlass. At the stoplight at Carpenter Road, I watched in the rearview as it swung into a strip mall, then out through the exit into my lane, stopping a couple of cars back.

It didn't have to mean anything. It might have had nothing to do with Lieutenant Karyl enlisting all the neighboring departments to look for an ancient blue Oldsmobile fastback with my number on the plate. The prickling on the back of my neck could mean there was too much starch in my collar.

When the cruiser followed me onto I-94 West and then onto the State Street exit, I knew I'd moved up on Karyl's list. That meant he wasn't any closer to laying hands on Jerry Marcus than he had been, and he needed Holly Zacharias more than ever to smoke him out. He'd have checked all the flights, and probably thought I had her stashed somewhere instead of on a train to Chicago.

Anyway, that was the hope. As long as he kept the tag on me, the better her chances of her not opening the door of her father's house to the local constabulary.

After crossing Eisenhower Parkway, the lights flashed and the siren sounded, a brief warning growl. I pulled over. After the usual wait designed to make you sweat through the upholstery, both doors swung open and they came my way, walking in Quentin Tarantino slow-motion the way they do, hands resting on sidearms. They sandwiched me. I never saw the partner's face on the passenger's side, just his midsection in a crisp shirt and the junk wagon belt with all its paraphernalia. The one on my side was fortyish, with a brown moustache clipped military fashion, a pedal-shaped jaw, and the standard mirrored sunglasses.

"Good morning, Officer. There's a revolver in the glove compartment. I've got a permit."

He asked for it, along with my license, registration, and proof of insurance. He had a light Southern accent; Kentucky, maybe.

He looked at the stuff. "You're Amos Walker?"

I had a number of clever answers ready, none of them appropriate. I said I was.

"Get out of the car, please."

I did, and stood for the frisk, feet spread, leaning on my hands on the hood, while the faceless partner opened the glove compartment.

Kentucky said, "Will you follow us, please?"

"I'm not under arrest?"

"Someone just wants to see you. If you prefer, you can ride in the cruiser and Officer Brindle will follow in your car."

I elected to drive.

We headed downtown, as of course we would. I switched on the radio. There was a traffic update, then the weather, then a teaser promising an important new development in the Ann Arbor murder, after the station break. The light baritone at the mike made it sound like he was reporting the results of a contest.

"The Ann Arbor murder;" quaint. In Detroit we just assign them a number.

---

I slid the pointer all the way right and left, but the old conspiracy was still in place: All the stations had gone on break at the same time. I went back to the first. The news reader's voice, resonant and lighthearted, announced that the murder victim the Ann Arbor Police had identified as Jerry Marcus wasn't, despite DNA evidence that had seemed to confirm the matter, and that Marcus was now being sought for the murder. Who the victim was, and how modern forensic science had managed to confuse him with his killer, had turned a fairly routine killing into a mystery. It was no wonder this guy was having such a good time. Last night's Pistons victory was a letdown after that.

A woman at the next station I tuned into had more. Fingerprints and ballistics had established a direct connection between Marcus and the shooting of a bouncer in front of the Necto Nightclub early the previous morning.

None of this was new, of course; Karyl had sat on the details as long as he dared. Just like in a romantic comedy, you have to come clean before the woman finds it all out by herself, and the media is nothing if not a woman you had to court the old-fashioned way or plunge into a world of pain. But I listened to it all as if it were new, on the off-chance hearing it laid out by a stranger might trigger something. It didn't.

As I leaned over to switch off the radio, I spotted a gray minivan in my right-hand mirror, tailgating the car in the lane next to mine. I wouldn't have thought anything about it, except for the driver's curly head and elfin face.

Where he got the wheels didn't matter. Even an amateur movie director knows a little about a lot of things, and this one needed a trailer just to carry his IQ around.

His resemblance to the dead man was eerie. I felt a theory beginning to sprout, in the dark, like the eyes on a potato. It made as much sense as anything else in the case, and as much as anything else nothing at all.

# TWENTY-TWO

We turned off Main Street onto Fourth, a block short of the street where the police station stood. It wasn't a mistake; the Kentucky Kop signaled the turn a hundred yards ahead to make sure he didn't lose me. When two unoccupied meters came up, the cruiser swung into the curb. I took the one behind. When I got out, the officer who'd been driving pointed at my meter. I went back and cranked everything I had into it: For all I knew I wouldn't be back for not less than one year nor more than five.

So he was a company man. Only not so much he dropped a lousy two bits into his own meter; it was blinking red. I knew there was something about his moustache I didn't like.

He left his partner to monitor the radio and we walked south. The sun was bright, but our breath curled in the air. There were still some tank tops, shorts, and flip-flops about. I put my summer wear away in October, but it was a local thing. In Florida the polar coats and mukluks would have come out.

We'd lost the van, or it had lost us, at the last turn. I figured Jerry Marcus had found a space past the corner. Where he'd go from there was the first easy thing about this job.

At Washington we crossed to the other side. There was a barbecue place up ahead, with an orange neon sign. I asked who was buying.

The cop said nothing; he was as good as his moustache.

We passed the place. Just beyond it he opened a door and held it for me. He reached behind his back and brought out my Chief's Special in its clip. "He says you can have this back." He didn't follow me inside.

It was a bookstore, and from the smell it dealt in used books mostly. The smell was of fusty paper, desiccated bindings, and petrified library paste; dry rot, to the unromantic. Fetid. The atmosphere of an Egyptian tomb exposed to the sun after three thousand years.

I supposed; I'd never been closer than a midnight showing of *The Mummy*. It had its charms. I can read a book and let it go, but I'm not immune. Dead movie stars glowered out from posters and black-and-white stills hanging at Krazy Kat angles on the walls that weren't entirely covered with books. Somewhere a stereo was playing swing. In Ann Arbor it's possible to pass between three centuries in fifteen minutes.

Ancient writings. Archaic music. A place out of time.

A bookstore.

The layout was split-level. I climbed a short flight of steps to where a long-haired refugee from Woodstock looked up from behind a desk piled with old paperbacks. He wore a T-shirt with a ferret on it over a raveled sweatshirt. He would smell like the store, couldn't avoid it.

"Welcome to Aunt Agatha's," he said. "First time?"

"Yeah. What keeps the walls from collapsing into the basement?"

He took me literally. "Previous owner had them double-reinforced." His voice fell to a whisper. "It used to be an adult bookstore."

"The hell you say."

"Can I help you find anything?"

I slid a cigarette into my mouth. "I'm looking for a man."

"Uh, this isn't the place for that. Also there's no smoking."

"I'm just gumming it. The man I'm looking for is named Karyl; looks like the third guy from the left in the evolution chart?"

He paled a shade. I followed his gaze to the back of the store, where the lieutenant was flipping through the pages of something with a woman undressing on the glossy cover. She wore scarlet lipstick and black underwear. There was more of her in various hair colors and varieties of nudity on the walls, blown up to poster size. The artists must have ordered their pink paint by the barrel and applied it with a roller.

"This is where I like to spend my lunch hour," Karyl said, slipping the book back into its slot on a shelf. "I love a good mystery."

"I thought you professionals made fun of them."

"Not me. They help take my mind off work. My wife thinks I'm ruggedly handsome, by the way."

"I can see it." I grinned. "I had to take the last couple nights out on somebody. I figured if I got you mad enough you'd finish me off clean."

"That's not how we work here."

"It was a joke, Lieutenant."

"You're a funny guy. Especially behind the wheel."

"I bet Blue Ford went straight to the airport."

"*Both* airports; and his name is Barlow. We got him straight off the mayor's detail in Detroit, and cheap: Enough is enough, you know?"

"More than enough," I said. "It's a great place for someone like me to work."

"I can see that. Barlow kind of liked you when you told him where you were going that first time, but I think that's changed. He practically had to get a warrant to find out that no one answering the Zacharias girl's description boarded a plane at either Metro or Coleman. Airline people these days are worse than lifers when it comes to prying anything out of them."

He opened a door in the back wall.

"Sign says EMPLOYEES ONLY," I said.

"The owners are old friends."

A storeroom half the size of the shop had two-by-four shelves all the way to the ceiling, stuffed tight with books, but the inventory had outgrown the space sometime around Appomattox. The place looked as if Paul Bunyan had picked it up and given it a shake. Apart from the necessary aisles for foot traffic there wasn't a square foot of unused space, and the books piled on the floor leaned against each other like a gang of drunks holding themselves up. We embroidered our way between knee-high stacks, cleared off a pair of folding metal chairs, and sat facing each other. Department regulations would require Karyl shaved daily, but his chin was blue already. If you watch a Slav closely enough you can actually see his whiskers grow.

"I guess you want to know why I didn't put out a warrant for your arrest."

"It wouldn't be that you like me despite my quirky sense of humor."

"I like your quirky sense of humor better than I like you. You've got a rep for clamming up tight as a cell door when the cell doors come out."

I looked around the room. "If you thought this would be less intimidating than the county lockup, you're full of hooey. Just being surrounded by all these perfect solutions brings out all my childhood feelings of inadequacy."

"Everything comes in threes in those stories, did you notice? The third key always opens the lock. Only there's never a lock where we live. When there is one it leads to shit. Put away that fucking cigarette."

I poked it back into the pack.

"Your girlfriend's father picked her up at Union Station in Chicago last night," he said.

"Thanks for the information. One time I was stuck in

Niles overnight when the engineer hit a cow. I wouldn't ask my ex-wife to spend a night in Niles. Why did they ever get rid of cowcatchers?"

"We think about trains, too; just not right away. I told you I read a lot of mysteries. I know stupid cops and smart cops. A department full of smart cops is too much to hope for, but one full of stupid cops like you find in a lot of these stories would fall apart in a year. Do you have any idea how long the Ann Arbor Police Department has been in existence?"

"No."

"Me neither, but it's longer than a year. I've been on it eight. It's a college town. On this shift alone, ten officers are studying for the bar; I'm practically a legal aide by osmosis. You realize by smuggling a material witness across state lines you turned a simple case of obstruction into a federal beef?"

"I hear they feed you good in the Milan pen."

"Shut the fuck up. I said I cut you a break by not having you brought here in cuffs. I don't give those out twice in one day."

I reached for my cigarette pack. "I think better when this is in my mouth."

"You should never take it out."

I slid it into place. "You gave me a break, I'll give you one back. I was on my way here to do that anyway. Send a couple of plainclothesmen up this street a couple of blocks. You'll find Marcus in a doorway."

He went on looking at me without twitching a muscle. Cops are trained to get answers without asking questions.

"A doorway," I went on, "or an alley, or dressed up like a mailbox; someplace he can wait for me to come back to my car without attracting attention. He followed me here. Can I keep him?"

Nothing; wrong room. I changed the subject. "I laid over in a dump in Ypsi. He picked me up somewhere between there and where I got pulled over."

"Why Ypsi?"

"It was better than jail."

"You don't know the town. Keep talking. I'll tell you when it starts to make sense."

"I wish you would. I've seen cartoons in the *New Yorker* that made more.

"I was so busy looking out for that damn blue Ford I didn't notice I was pulling a second shadow," I said. "I'm a crack detective, Lieutenant; I can find my reading glasses when they're on the end of my nose. Marcus wants Holly as much as you do. I'm supposed to lead him to her. That's been my part right along. I'm just that sap you read about in those books you like so much. Without the fall guy they'd be over in a hundred pages."

"You must have lost him when you lost my man or Marcus would be in Chicago. How'd he pick you back up?"

"A lucky shot, maybe; say he staked out the interstate from the airport, looking for my ride. He's that kind of a fanatic. You can ask him."

"I've got some other things to ask him first," Karyl said. "Starting with why he killed his brother."

I took the cigarette out of my mouth, reversed ends. The first was as wet as my armpits.

"His brother," I said.

A muscle twitched then, near a corner of his mouth. Somewhere in East Asia a mountain slid into a village: It all had something to do with a butterfly. I'm not that kind of smart.

"This isn't a hobby," he said. "We've been working the case. It gave us something to do while we were waiting for you to swoop in and tie it all up."

I struck a match. The whole damn store could burn down for all I cared.

"Oh, I knew there had to be a brother involved. A twin, in fact."

I lit my cigarette while he waited. The smoke cleared my head in direct opposition to my lungs.

"DNA," I said. "Stands for Don't Know Anything. I'm an expert on that."

# TWENTY-THREE

The overage hippie came into the room, apologizing, glowered at my smoking cigarette, rummaged among the stock, and left carrying a stack of books under each arm with Post-it Notes sticking out from between pages. He kicked the door shut behind him. We said nothing until we were alone. Then Karyl took a cell from an inside pocket.

He gave orders for two minutes, repeating them for clarity, giving no explanation.

Just before he hung up—if you could call it that—he said, "What's waiting for a wash?" Then: "Use it."

He tapped the antenna against his teeth. "If Marcus doesn't show, I will feed you to the feds."

"He's hung around this long just to eliminate the only witness against him. He'll keep—if those Ypsi cops aren't still hanging around."

"When Ypsi said they were bringing you here, I told them to beat it after. By now there's an unmarked unit in the Kerrytown parking lot, with a clear view up Fourth. If he sticks out his head, there's a circus wagon around the corner, out of sight. We'll have his nuts in a cracker."

"I hope you're not using the blue Ford. I spotted it right away. I don't remember what I scored on my SATs, but it wasn't nineteen-fifty."

"It'll be the same make, but a different color. You heard what I said at the end."

I nodded. "Cop cars are supposed to sparkle. A little mud is as good as a brown paper bag. Rust would be better; but we can't have that here, can we?"

"I'll catch enough hell just over the mud. How'd you figure Marcus was a twin?"

"Something I heard once, about genes. But you broke the case; you tell it."

"We knew he had a brother building a bridge in Indonesia—he's an engineer, serving with the Peace Corps—but we didn't know he was back till yesterday. His mother didn't know, when we finally reached her in North Dakota. She hasn't heard from either of them since they left home years ago; something about some guy she started seeing after their father died, and blah-blah. She's the one who told us they were twins. We didn't know that either.

"Identical twins have identical DNA," he went on. "That's what you heard, I guess."

"What about Forensics? They miss class that day?"

"They printed the room, of course, and matched some of them to the stiff. Prints, that's something twins *don't* share. What most of these books leave out is just how many different sets a place picks up, from visitors and such, and how many of them are never identified. Neither brother had ever been arrested or served in the military, so the FBI database came up empty. When we get Jerry, we'll know everything he touched in that room and sort it all out."

He stopped tapping his teeth. "Without a twin in the picture, I guess anybody can make a mistake. The dead man looked like Jerry, it was Jerry's apartment. When the blood samples checked out against the saliva on some unwashed glasses, follicles and skin cells in the bed, urine traces in the toilet, the report practically wrote itself."

"What was the brother's name?"

His mouth made something resembling a smile. "Tom."

I had to laugh. "They had a legitimate beef against their old lady before she took up dating."

"Could've been worse. Could've been Bugs and Daffy. So now we knew it was Tom's head with a slug through it. After the Bismarck cops spoke to the mother, we checked with the Peace Corps. He finished the bridge and flew home first of August. We figure he came to see Jerry, or Jerry lured him to his place. There he killed Tom and rabbited with the money he got off his investors. *He* knew about twins and genes. As long as we thought he was the victim, he was free to start up again someplace else with his getaway stake."

" 'Getaway stake,' " I said. "You *do* read detective stories."

"Love 'em. Most of the ones I read were written before they cracked the code. He'd planned it a while. It was kind of refreshing, actually. We usually find our murderers sitting in the same room with their victims, waiting for us to come calling."

"You still think it was all for money?"

"Con artists are charming rogues at the cineplex. Most of them are supporting dope habits and worse. They'd as soon kill their pigeons as pluck them. Then they run."

"Jerry didn't."

"I said he was smart," Karyl said. "I didn't say he wasn't nuts. He decided what he'd done wasn't clever enough, traced you and Holly to the Necto, and took a shot at her, which if it hadn't been for that lug of a bouncer would've left no one to place him at the murder scene, carrying a box just like the one we knew he used to suppress the noise of gunfire when he killed Tom. Ballistics got a positive on the slug we took out of the bouncer. It matched the one in the apartment."

"How many psychopathic geniuses can one university turn out?"

"Two's the limit. After that we get mad."

My cigarette had gone out; they'll do that when you forget to draw on them. I peeled it off my lip and tossed it in a corner. "There's more to it than fraud."

"You *have* been busy," he said. "Why don't I just give everyone downtown the day off and let you cap this one off by yourself?"

I couldn't help but think he was being sarcastic, so I didn't answer. "I talked to Alec Moselle yesterday."

"Detail I assigned to you reported you holed up in his trailer a half hour. I thought you were trying to duck it."

"So you know him."

He rolled his eyes.

"Some guys never get over those African issues of *National Geographic.* He's a pain, but not in the neck of my division. Personally I think we've got better things to do than lock people up for flashing their tits and wienies in public. If we stopped, so would he. I got my son to stop cussing like a sailor when he was five years old by ignoring him. Moselle's number came up on Marcus' redial. He told us he broke up the partnership when Jerry turned dirty. He turned him down when he put the arm on him for an investment in *Mr. Alien Elect.*"

"That's not why they broke up. Moselle was covering his own ass when he told you that. They met in the U of M film program; Moze cowrote the *Alien* script. Jerry rewrote the ending to take place in the Michigan Theater."

"That doesn't sound bad enough to dissolve the partnership."

"It wasn't a case of professional differences. He planned to blow up the place for real."

"Why'd he want to do that?"

I jumped a little. I'd never heard Karyl bark before.

"Jerry's first student film got panned there when he showed it. You know about the Cinema Slam."

"Crowd control's worst headache, after the art fairs. You buy what Moselle said? He's more slippery than one of his models covered in Vaseline."

"I can't come up with a reason he'd make it up. He said

Jerry showed him a barn filled with bags of fertilizer out in farm country. Fertilizer, Lieutenant."

He stood and pecked keys on his phone.

"Karyl. Pick up Alec Moselle. Start with his studio on Washtenaw, but get out a BOLO at the same time. Yeah, him. No. Christ. Who gives a shit about that?"

He banged shut the antenna and looked at me. "How come I'm only hearing about this now?"

"Slow down," I said. "That was years ago. When those planes flew into the World Trade Center, Jerry backed off. Moze said he helped him dump the bags in a swamp. After that they broke up and Moselle swapped a conspiracy charge for nuisance citations. But a case could be made for the first for not reporting it at the time. Why would Marcus think he could squeeze money out of him, if he didn't threaten blackmail? Moze says he hung up on him, but when you bring him in you can ask him yourself if he called his bluff. Fifty grand was cheap compared with what the feds brought against everyone involved in the Oklahoma City bombing."

He got back on his cell. "Karyl. Cancel the BOLO. We'll pay him a social call instead." He broke the connection. "No sense haring in there Code Three. Artists are sensitive." He smacked the phone against his palm. "What put you onto him in the first place?"

"Redial, same thing as you. I know all about these here telephone gizmos."

His phone rang. The tone was the *Peter Gunn* score.

He listened, said, "Stay put. He might show yet."

"Moze?" I asked, when he was through talking.

"Marcus. There was no sign of a van answering your description. Those officers from Ypsilanti must have spooked him finally."

"Either that, or he figured out where Holly wound up."

"Let's hope. Chicago P.D. has more cops around her father's place than the mayor, all in plainclothes. I don't mind sharing the credit. As a matter of—"

*Peter Gunn* thundered again. I knew I'd be hearing it the rest of the day.

I could hear the tinny voice on the other end. I recognized Alec Moselle's address on Washtenaw.

". . . shots fired."

I hit the street just behind Karyl. He looked up the north end of the street, brought one arm around in a long loop. Headlights came on. A late-model gray Ford crusted with old mud spun away from the curb and stopped alongside us in ten seconds. The lieutenant sprinted around to the passenger's side and got in. No one said I couldn't, so I swung open the back door and climbed in behind the driver.

"Crank it up!" Karyl said. "Twenty-three south."

"Code Three?"

"Fuck yeah!"

The cop behind the wheel flipped on the siren and popped the clutch. Our start threw me back so hard I felt the spare in the trunk against my kidneys. We made a howling right against the light, scattering jaywalkers like crows.

# TWENTY-FOUR

We swept our lane clear of traffic all the way down Main Street and entered US-23 with two wheels to spare. I scrambled into a seat belt somewhere between ninety-five and a hundred, but that speed was history when we came up on the Washtenaw Avenue exit. At the bottom of the ramp we skinned left on the far edge of the yellow.

The light was red at Carpenter, with the eastbound lanes blocked solid, but we didn't brake, slaloming into the opposite lane and swinging back into the right a centimeter short of a city bus waiting at the light. I waited for the driver to blast his airhorn, forgetting for the moment the vehicle I was riding in. We continued at expressway speed along one of the busiest streets in the city, smearing the scenery on both sides like an angry artist swiping his turpentine rag across wet oils. A cataract of potholes loosened a filling in one of my molars.

I leaned forward. "Can we stop at a drugstore? I'm out of cigarettes."

Nothing. Just as well; my voice fluttered up and down the scale. I pushed my imaginary brake pedal deep into the floorboards with both feet.

A bicyclist glanced back at us, twisted his handlebars, and bounded up over the curb, nailing the landing in a Park 'n' Ride. I almost applauded.

We took a piece off the curb swinging into the parking lot of the strip mall where Alec Moselle developed his nude-scapes on the upper deck. Ann Arbor Police cruisers were parked in an orderly row in front of the line of shops, their lights flashing red and blue. Our driver found the brakes then, laying down four permanent black patches on the asphalt while the gasoline whomped around inside the tank. We'd stopped square between the yellow lines.

"Nice." Karyl's voice was as calm as a deejay's on a classical station. "Try to pare off a couple of seconds next time."

"Crate needs a tune-up." Our driver yanked the key out of the ignition.

The lieutenant laid his elbow on the back of his seat and looked back at me.

"You all right? You look a little green."

The son of a bitch sounded pleased with himself.

"I can't recommend the steak-and-eggs at the Chicken Palace," I said.

"Where are my manners? Amos Walker, Officer Kinderly. Three generations at Daytona."

Kinderly reached back a hand. I pried my fingers out of the back of the front seat and took it. He had a long upper lip and a reddish moustache you could wipe off with a towel. "The lieutenant's a jokester. I just got my learner's permit."

Cop humor. They'd drain the brake fluid from a wheelchair just for kicks.

"Thanks for the boogie ride," I said. "Can we go again?"

I had to wait until Kinderly came around and opened my door. There are no handles in the perp's seat. I got out on rubber legs.

A half-dozen radios buzzed and crackled between scraps of sentences that buzzed and crackled also. The usual gang of spectators had gathered, but the local gawkers were housebroken; they stood at a respectful distance, watching a uniform unwind yellow tape from a fat roll.

"Everything seems in hand," Karyl said, tugging down the hem of his suitcoat. "Guess there was no hurry after all."

I got it then; I'm pretty quick when you drop a safe on my head. Eleven and a half minutes from Fourth Street to Washtenaw Avenue was the price of obstruction of justice and just generally being a pain in the ass of appointed authority. I entered it in my commonplace book.

The officer guarding the steps to the second story recognized the lieutenant. He nodded a greeting, no salute. That department would respect Casual Friday.

"How bad?" Karyl said.

"It don't get any worse, L.T." He drew a finger across his throat.

"Doesn't. Who's in charge?"

"Sergeant Rogers."

"Who's he?"

"Ypsi Township."

"A pro. Good."

"Bad mix, that beat," Kinderly told me; we'd bonded, it looked like. "Harlem and Louisville, fighting Bull Run every Saturday night."

"Did the lieutenant tell you I'm from Detroit?"

"Point taken. Any openings?"

"Only every Saturday night."

The reception area looked the same as yesterday, plastered with poster-size pictures in black and white of people in open areas, without clothes. He'd taken some down, added others: an unbroken sea of flesh. I couldn't figure it. Even Picasso had burned out on the Blue Period after a while.

One thing had changed. The door behind the doughnut-shaped counter that operated by manipulating a woman's mammary stood open. Myra, the receptionist, stood outside the doughnut, sobbing out a statement to a scribbling officer in uniform and a plainclothesman half Karyl's age, wearing tweeds over a V-neck sweater and a tie printed all over with wolverines. Myra had exchanged her Route 66 muumuu for a horizontally striped blouse just as loose, with the tail out over faded jeans, relaxed-fit to accommodate a pair of hips that would feed a cannibal village for a week. The arrows shaved into the base of her red woodpecker crest needed trimming; the stubble was brown.

Karyl showed his shield to the man in tweeds. They shook hands.

"Looks like robbery," Sergeant Rogers said. "These places have a lot of expensive chemicals and equipment you can turn into cash quick as a cashier's check. We'll turn 'em up even quicker; we know all the places. Only reason they're still in business is if we shut them down we'd have to start all over again from scratch."

Karyl pumped a fist up and down. "Fast-forward, Sergeant. This isn't the class tour."

"Sorry. Perp walked straight past the desk and into the back. Receptionist got up to stop him, heard shots, and called nine-one-one. Dispatch told her get out. She hung out on the deck, then went back inside. Just what part of 'Get out'"—he shifted gears before a glower straight out of Transylvania—"Back door open. Place upside down, her boss on the floor with two bullets in him. Still breathing, she thought, but not for long. Not long enough anyway to say diddly. No sign of the perp.

"We got a description," he added.

Karyl looked as interested as a husband listening to the wife's day. He walked around him, inserted himself between the scribbling officer and the receptionist, drew a rolled-up photograph from an inside pocket, and spread it between both hands, six inches in front of her face. He showed enormous control while she wailed, blew her nose into a limp wad of Kleenex, then nodded.

"Out loud," he said, not unkindly. "County prosecutor's a dick on details."

"That's the man." A phlegmy whisper.

The lieutenant showed the picture to Rogers.

"You got one of these at roll call, yes?"

"Yes, sir."

"Suspect Jerome Marcus, brother of Thomas, deceased. Wanted for murder and attempted. Armed, extremely dangerous. Last seen driving gray minivan, may have dumped it by now for something else."

Rogers jerked his chin at the officer with the notebook, who flipped a page and scribbled.

"What are you waiting for, the Rose Parade? Call it in. Jesus Christ. They told me you were with Ypsi."

The sergeant's face went blank.

"Drug killings, L.T. Passion killings. Guy-wiggles-his-eyebrows-at-your-girl killings. Wifie-runs-over-hubby-with-her-SUV-over-his-chippie killings. I got a ten-year-old kid killed his six-year-old sister with a Luger their uncle left loaded on the top shelf of his closet, like he thought that was Mount Everest. Nudie photog shot dead in his studio? Fuck you—with all respect, *Lieutenant.*" He took out a cell while the uniform barked into a microphone hooked to a shoulder strap.

Karyl blinked at Rogers. "Feel better?"

"A little."

They shook hands again.

Cops.

"Okay," Karyl said. "Let's see the dessert tray."

We went through the door into Alec Moselle's photography studio. The room took up most of the shop's footage, with all the standard paraphernalia in place, arranged in the standard state of clutter, a letdown after the carnal display out front.

Someone, presumably the first cop on the scene, had drawn up one of the black shades that covered the windows to let light in. Combined with the fluorescents in the ceiling, the sun made the room obscenely bright, with all the cold shadowless efficient artificiality of a county morgue.

A black-and-silver camera on a tripod, a flat covered in blue fabric, lights on aluminum stands, white umbrella reflectors tilted every which way, a tall stool for the model to sit; a stone-lithograph table older than the building, rescued, probably, from a defunct printshop—cluttered with X-Acto knives, discarded blades, and scraps of photo paper cropped from negatives and positives, cross-lit by natural-light bulbs in gooseneck lamps, still burning with a slight sizzling noise like bacon frying in the next room.

More cameras—motor-driven Polaroids, steel-cased Nikons, Kodak Instamatics, sleek pocket-size digitals, a black-box Speed Graphic, the kind newspaper photographers used in old movies, lay about on low tables and the tops of cabinets among disembodied lenses, aluminum canisters, and Polaroid shots curled like empty chrysalides. An ancient thing of burnished oak and brushed steel mounted on bamboo legs stood aloof in a corner, complete with a black shroud for the photographer to duck under, hold up his hodful of magnesium powder and a rubber squeeze-ball to set it off: *Watch the birdie!*

Smocks and costumes, a full suit of medieval armor, cowboy hats, top hats, bowler hats, straw hats, picture hats, slouch hats, all kinds of hats: wizard's conicals, Mexican sombreros, caps, berets, cloches, Easter bonnets, homburgs, fedoras, trilbies, Tyroleans, tri-colored beanies with propellers: Heaven, to the bald man. Stage properties enough to furnish a community theater through every production from *My Fair Lady* to *Sweeney Todd*: Pistols, swords, snuffboxes, codpieces, a human skull I took as plaster until I picked it up and a tooth fell out.

A working traffic signal flashed sequentially in red, yellow, and green; at the very least it broke up the flat bright light of a homicide scene.

The floor was linoleum, dirty, and worn through to the subflooring in leprous patches. Alec Moselle—"Moze" to his public—lay on it as if he were just another prop.

He was sprawled on his back, one leg flung casually across the other, like a man relaxing in an armchair. He'd been shot twice in the chest, but he hadn't bled much, because one of the bullets had stopped his heart. There was a sharp powder stench in the air, fading by the second.

Oh, and he was nude.

A tie-dyed T-shirt lay in a heap atop carpenter's jeans with an empty loop designed to hold a hammer. Gray undershorts, a crumpled pair of white tube socks, and a worn pair of Reeboks had been flung into a corner; *flung* was the word that came first to mind. There is something about the evidence of undressing that says everything about whether it was performed by the person who had been wearing the clothes or someone else.

Karyl saw what I saw the moment I saw it. He pointed at the T-shirt. "Blood. The motherfucker stripped him after he killed him. Nothing like a psychopath with a sense of irony."

The police photographer's flash flooded the corpse at just that second.

"Moze's masterpiece," I said. "I should've bought one of his originals yesterday. I could've retired."

"On behalf of law enforcement everywhere, I wish to hell you had." Karyl turned away, rubbing his hands. "What else we got?"

Plenty, as it turned out.

# TWENTY-FIVE

T his is how the uniforms found the place," Sergeant Rogers said. "Looks like he put up a fight."

"How many photographer murders have you investigated?" Karyl asked.

"This makes one."

"All their studios are mare's nests. Yes?" He lifted his heavy brows at Myra.

"It's always like this." Her Kleenex was disintegrating. The officer who'd been taking her statement produced a nifty little cellophane packet of tissues and gave it to her. It was the damnedest department I'd ever seen.

"Always running around, snatching up lenses and fresh rolls of film, monkeying with their lights and reflectors," Karyl said. "Plenty of time to tidy up later. Only Moze didn't have a later."

He poked the square toe of a shoe at a brass shell casing on the linoleum. "Magnum round, I'm guessing. He's getting careless, forgetting to pick up after himself and not bothering anymore about the noise. Normally that's a good sign."

"I don't like it," I said.

"Me neither. When a nice neat killer forgets himself, it means he's coming unglued. What's in there?"

The plainclothesman followed his pointing finger to a narrow open door in back, shingled all over with Polaroids. "Darkroom, L.T. It's a mess too. We figured our thief ransacked it for equipment and chemicals, stuff he could turn into cash; but Bonaparte there's a dabbler, and says everything that should be there still is."

A black officer built like a linebacker, only too short by six inches, nodded when Karyl looked at him. "I do friends' weddings and like that, sir. I squeak by, but I can't afford half the stuff he's got. Had."

The lieutenant stepped into the darkroom, stepped out a second later. "No good. Place is a wreck."

"But if all photographers are as messy as you say—"

He cut Rogers off. "Never in their darkrooms. They're as tidy as Aunt Tillie in there."

Bonaparte said, "That's right. I was too busy checking out the supplies and equipment to think about it. You have to move fast once the stuff's in the soup. Can't afford to bump into stuff and waste time looking for things. Our victim wouldn't tear up his own place unless he was desperate."

Karyl looked around. "Anybody we know answers that description?"

I wandered over to another door standing open, on the other side of the model setup. It was an outside door. Gridded steel steps led down to a stretch of gray asphalt where Moselle had parked the ten-foot Airstream trailer he took out on location. I went down to it. The door was unlocked.

A mug with a photo screen-printed on it of a sea of naked flesh—probably one of his—stood on the table in the dinette area with the tag of a tea bag hanging outside the rim and some greenish-brown grains pasted inside at the bottom. It was the only thing that hadn't been there before, or anyway that I'd noticed. I tried reading the tea leaves, but I needed Lieutenant Karyl's Gypsy blood for that.

Just to be thorough I swung open a couple of doors mounted at floor level, looked at what was inside, and shut them. Empty.

I had a thought, almost; it was stillborn.

I went back upstairs, shaking my head. It might come back, or not. I'd worn all the whorls off my brain, and lost gripping power.

The uniform with the notebook was escorting Myra into the studio with a hand cupped under her elbow. She made a whimpering noise when they passed Moselle's body, but he patted her arm and took her into the darkroom. Karyl was back inside.

"What's he keep in these cabinets?"

I leaned in for a look. The room was no bigger than a half-bath, with a pair of stainless-steel sinks, shelves like the ones in the trailer, all in use, and some sleek black electronics, including an enormous copy camera for blow-ups that took up most of the space. A plastic clothesline with some glistening photographic prints still pinned to it dangled by only one hook above the sink; it had come loose from the hook opposite and hung nearly to the floor, which was littered with similar prints that had probably come loose from it when it fell or was torn loose. Bottles of developing fluid stood and lay on their sides in both sinks and there was an eye-stinging stench of solvent; an expensive spill, I thought.

The receptionist was looking at a built-in recess under the sink. The steel doors that belonged to it were flayed open. The cabinet was empty.

"Big plastic jugs." Her voice wobbled. "I don't remember what was on the labels. He said he kept them there because if he dropped one taking it down from above, he'd blow up the building. I thought he was joking." She started sobbing again.

"Magnesium and silver nitrate."

Everyone looked at Sergeant Bonaparte.

"Obsolete process," he said, "but some photogs still use it for artistic effect. They have to know what they're doing, though. He wasn't joking. Magnesium powder's what they used to call flash powder; goes up faster than gunpowder at the touch of a match. Silver nitrate is a rapid oxidant; they stopped using it in photography because it was self-destructive. Mix the two and you won't need the match. A gallon of each could take out the block."

The thought came back. It was a breech birth.

"He had more in his trailer."

Now everyone was looking at me.

"Just a guess. I checked it out just now. Every shelf was packed tight, like here, but a floor cabinet was empty. I didn't make the connection. Space is limited in a trailer. You need every inch, like in here. So why waste it? Last time I visited, he warned me against lighting a cigarette in there. He even patted the cabinet."

"They're big jugs."

Myra had taken center stage again. She'd begun to take a clinical interest. "He couldn't carry them far on foot. He came in the front, and no one drove out of that part of the lot while I was outside."

I felt an icy breath on the back of my neck. "Where did Moselle park his truck?"

"Truck? Oh, the pickup. In back, always. He used it to pull the trailer."

"Ford F-150, black, last year's model," I said. "It isn't there. Just the trailer."

Karyl glared at the woman. "Plate number."

"Forget that," I said. "I know where he's headed."

# PART FOUR

# CINEMA SLAM

# TWENTY-SIX

I t's a rush whenever an entire city rears up on its hind legs.

I'd seen it only a couple of times, during the dragnet for Gross, Turkel, and Smith, accused of ambushing Detroit Police officers, and when Charlotte Sing was wanted internationally for murder, narcotics, and trafficking in stolen human organs.

But when a quiet college town goes on the alert, the sirens seem louder, the flashing lights brighter, and the radio transmissions harsher. The same energy that goes into rooting for the Michigan football team spins square around on its axis and applies itself to an arrest, and fast.

For a few minutes, everyone with a two-way radio was on the air. Calls went downtown, to Washtenaw County sheriff's headquarters on Hogback (I'm not the one who names these streets), to the state police in Lansing, and to Detroit, ordering bomb squads and Early Response teams; that's SWAT, to you. An aerial shot of southeastern Michigan would show hordes of toy-size squad cars zeroing in on Ann Arbor like reverse ripples in a pond.

If the pilot could get clearance to take off: Helicopter rotors from all four departments and the U of M hospital medivac walloped the air, kicking up dust from construction sites and buzzing every window in its frame for miles.

I was back in the unmarked gray Ford, digging finger holes in the upholstery between Sergeants Rogers and Bonaparte, with Karyl seated in front beside Officer Kinderly and his lead foot. Our siren joined the kiyoodling wave, and we parted traffic like Moses on a souped-up snowplow.

"All this didn't have to happen." Karyl's voice was taut. "You knew Moselle was a likely target, Walker. He had too much on Marcus."

"I warned him. It didn't take. He was spooky about cops; he spent most of his working capital bailing his models out of jail and paying fines. He'd have spotted any detail you put on him and screamed it from the bell tower. Anyway, he said Marcus gave up his plans to blow up the theater. He was pretty convincing. And Jerry was still hot on Holly. She was ground zero then."

"We all had him wrong." But he didn't sound as if he were shifting any burdens. "Marcus swindled his investors not to get rich, but to raise cash to buy explosives. He dumped that fertilizer when Moselle didn't go along. Had to, if he was going to convince Moze not to turn him in after he had a chance to think about it."

"Then why kill his twin brother before he gathered what he needed?" I asked. "This guy's got the smarts to work everything out ten moves ahead. Why jump the gun so that he had to steal the stuff he needed after killing Moselle?"

"I've got a theory about that. You said the Marcuses' own mother didn't know Tom was back in the States. Maybe he dropped in on Jerry early, and *that* forced his hand. He tried to buy time by eliminating the only witness who could place him at the murder scene, carrying just the kind of box we'd be looking for once we worked out his M.O. When he saw you trailing cops, he realized he'd be committing murder in front of that many more, and shifted his focus. Moze was still a threat, and a guy that makes movies would know all about the chemicals his old partner worked with. Jerry already knew how to make a bomb, on account of his special-effects training; Moselle told you that much."

I watched the blur of scenery. I had the spooky feeling it was the one doing the moving while I sat still in the middle of it.

"It fits," I said.

"Fuckin' A, it fits."

"It fits so tight it stinks."


It stank as much as a madman could make it.

It should have been simple, as simple a thing as just another fast-shovel artist pulling the wool over the eyes of a couple of overripe hippies with dollar signs spinning around their heads. It didn't have to be about a spoiled genius unappreciated in his own time, with a running sore in his ego, a rotten spot in his brain, and an expert knowledge of demolitions.

That wasn't enough, though. It had to throw in a twin brother.

Science-fiction buffs know a lot about science fact. DNA is unique to the individual, except in the case of identical twins. Who knew at what point Jerry Marcus remembered that, and saw the whole thing laid out in front of him like a GPS map?

"Jerry was right-handed, wasn't he?" I asked.

Karyl kept his eyes on the street ahead. "Our graphologist says so: Forward slanting hand in the scribbles we found in his room. What's it got to do with anything?"

"Only that I'm an idiot. I could have tied this whole thing up that first day."

"Entertain me."

"I looked at the watch. If in the struggle with his killer it got smashed, we'd have time of death; unless, of course, the killer shattered it on purpose, to give himself an alibi."

"That one's got whiskers. We'd've suspected it straight off. I told you I read mysteries."

"I overlooked the most important thing: the wrist he wore it on. Right-handers usually wear it on the left, the non-working one. Otherwise it can get in the way of a physical project, or take too much of a beating and stop. This one was on the corpse's right wrist. It's inconclusive, but it suggests the man wearing it was left-handed."

"Well, when we nail Jerry, we'll see which hand he uses to sign his confession."

"I read somewhere that twins are reversed that way: One's right-handed, the other left. In extreme cases, even their hearts are reversed. Anything there?"

"Seems to me the M.E. would have said something. She's a witch, but she's as thorough as my proctologist."

"I guess it's not universal. Fingerprints, being right- or left-handed; the old-fashioned boys with their hunches never ruled them out. The trouble with all this jazzy new science is we put it in front of what worked before."

We'd bogged down at the old bugaboo at Carpenter Road; a tractor-trailer rig had come to a stop this side of the crosswalk, leaving no room for anything wider than a bicycle to thread its way through the space. Kinderly sat drumming his fingers on the wheel. Karyl leaned hard left, shoving the pedal into the block. The engine whined against the pressure of the brake.

The driver got the message. He let up, spun the wheel right, and bucked up onto the grassy berm. We took out a sign advertising a charity car wash. It plastered itself to the windshield until he kicked it loose with the wipers.

I was getting used to that stretch of expressway, although I figured it would seem tame at a leisurely ninety.

Back on Main, over the torn-up railroad tracks, and Liberty again, turning jaywalkers into law-abiding citizens in a flash. Six blocks from the theater, an officer setting up a barricade scrambled out of our way; we might have sheared a button off his uniform.

We slowed finally, coasting to a stop a block from the action. When we got out, we were spectators.

Men and women in blue, some in combat fatigues, spilled like ants through doors on both sides of the street, blasting whistles and waving batons at the crowds they were herding out into the open. Something that resembled an armored personnel carrier trundled down the exact center of the street, blaring cautionary advice through a megaphone that sounded like a saxophone with a split reed. The usual cluster of half-wits were gathered on facing sidewalks, giving the tall-fingered salute and waving misspelled signs. A flying wedge of uniforms dashed them to pieces, scattering red Solo cups right and left. The tracked military vehicle ground a rolling bong into splinters.

The carrier stopped in front of Borders. A hatch opened up top, and from it swarmed humanoid creatures in riot gear—medieval-looking helmets with smoked-glass visors, gas masks, and quilted catchers' vests, automatic weapons slung from webbed straps across their shoulders. It was like watching clowns pour out of a car in the circus.

Karyl flashed his gold shield, stopping a Golem in Kevlar in mid-sprint. He plucked out an earpiece to hear what the lieutenant was saying, then nodded and pointed in the direction of the Michigan Theater. Its marquee was flashing, advertising a revival showing of *The Age of Innocence*: Good picture. The Ford F-150 Jerry Marcus had stolen from Alec Moselle was parked in front. We sprinted that way.

The crowd gathered under the marquee was strictly of-
ficial: radios buzzed, bullhorns bawled. A giant lugging an
assault rifle lifted his visor, exposing pale gray eyes in a face
black as a galosh. He nodded at Karyl's shield. "Lieutenant
Randolph. Detroit ERT."

"Thanks for coming out. Situation?"

"Hostage. Suspect stuck a gun in the ticket clerk's face
and dragged her into the projection room; where they show
the movies?"

"I know what a projection room is. Where are the other
employees?"

"Evacuated; all except the assistant manager; she's
been a big help. She said he shouted something about a
bomb."

"What do you know about it?"

"He was wearing a vest of some kind, and he's got a remote. I got men all over, at all the exits, but he's got the projector on. We can't get a clear shot against the bright light
without risking hitting the hostage."

"What about from outside?"

"I'll let Mrs. Candlemass explain that part. She's the assistant manager."

He led us inside through plate-glass doors framed in
chromium. From the gold-leaf lobby, mahogany staircases
swept up like smoke to a carpeted mezzanine. There were
frescoes in the arched ceiling panels, cherubim, lions
rampant; and that was just the lobby.

It crawled with cops. They stood on the carpeted steps
curving gracefully to the gilded balcony from two sides,
patrolled the balcony itself, surrounded a bronze drinking

fountain. Randolph called over a woman standing in a group of officers.

Mrs. Candlemass, the assistant manager, was a tall woman of about fifty, in a black sheaf dress with pearls and silver hair cut modishly. She wore makeup and pearl buttons in her ears. I figured she lived in the suburbs.

"The place was built thirty years before safety stock," she explained. "Before that, film was a combination of celluloid and silver nitrate; extremely volatile."

"Yeah," Karyl said. "I can't believe I never heard of silver nitrate before today. What about it?"

"That's just it. There were fires, fatalities until someone got the bright idea of enclosing the projection room in solid concrete."

"It's a bunker," Randolph said. "No outside windows."

"How'd the projectionist get out?"

"Through the door, if he moved quickly. They didn't always," the assistant manager added.

"Would the room contain a blast?"

"I suppose that would depend on the material. I don't know much about explosives."

He told her what was in Marcus' vest. The rouge on her cheeks stood out against her sudden pallor. She shook her head.

"Thank you." Sets of bronze doors were marked by illuminated aisle numbers. He took a step toward the closest door.

She said, "Your men will be careful, won't they? The Michigan's on the National Register of Historic Places."

He stopped. "I'd rather answer to them than the girl's parents. What's her name?"

"Crystal." She bit her lip.

The auditorium was only half the size of the one in the renovated Fox Theater in Detroit, but it seated more people than the average multiplex, and comfortably, in deep seats upholstered in tough, wine-colored mohair, with a chandelier ablaze, as was every light in the vaulted room, including wall sconces, the stumble-bulbs in the risers, and utility lamps for cleaning and maintenance crews. It was as bright as outdoors.

The place belonged to the days of Rudolph Valentino, Lon Chaney, Sr., and Ramon Novarro, with an apron in front of the screen deep enough to host a live show before the chariot races started onscreen, an orchestra pit, and a Wurlitzer organ wheezing accompaniment to Garbo, Gable, and all the Barrymores; it would dwarf any refugee from late-night live television, but it was just the right size for Randolph Scott, Marilyn Monroe, and the Marx brothers: faces made to fill a screen the size of a football field. Those places came with a hush, like a cathedral at Easter; only not today. Men and women in uniform prowled the aisles, leading bomb-sniffing dogs on halters and poking big black rubber flashlights between the seats.

A hard white shaft stretched from a square opening at the back of the room halfway up the wall, splashing the movie screen. I shielded my eyes with my hand, but I couldn't see anything beyond it. He'd taken the highest ground possible, and a point of vantage from where he could see everything that happened below.

Lieutenant Randolph jerked his shoulder toward one of the gilded walls, where a thin rectangle outlined the door to the stairs leading to the projection room. "They've been up there twenty minutes. We haven't heard a peep."

*Marcus might have been waiting for our entrance.* A shot rang around the acoustically designed room and one of the bulbs in the chandelier burst and showered a glittering powder of glass onto the seats below.

Peep.

# TWENTY-SEVEN

We hit the deck, groping for our weapons. The carpet smelled of Jujubes. I looked at Lieutenant Karyl, lying belly-down beside me in the aisle. "Okay if I go out for popcorn?"

He said nothing; until I started crawling around back in the direction we'd come. A hand strung with steel cable clamped on my arm.

"What the hell do you think you're doing?"

His whisper was as loud as another man's bellow.

"Cover me." I looked back over my shoulder and grinned. "I always wanted to say that."

He had more to bring to the conversation, but a report from the projection room cut him off. The bullet took a shard of polished mahogany off the arm of a seat a few inches above our heads, exposing yellow wood.

He let go of me, raised himself on one elbow, leveled the barrel of his semiautomatic across his other wrist, and squeezed the trigger.

He'd aimed high because of the ticket clerk. The slug struck the smile off Cupid on the wing in a ceiling vault. By then I was scrambling on hands and knees toward the exit.

One of the heavy doors was held open by a hinged prop. I kicked the prop loose with my foot as I crawled through the opening. The door glided shut against the pressure of a pneumatic tube, but not before another shot aimed from up high struck a panel. Painted plaster dust pelted my back.

Okay, so it wasn't bronze. You can't trust anything in show business. Karyl or one of the other cops returned fire.

One of the armored officers on point in the lobby came my way, shouldering his assault rifle, but he must have recognized me from when I came in with Karyl, because he swung it behind his back by its shoulder strap and bent to help me to my feet. I was halfway up; I waved him off.

"How do I get up to the projection room?"

His face was an indistinct oval behind the tinted shield. "I don't know. We're still waiting on a floor plan. Anybody hit?"

"Not yet, but somebody's going to be filling out a lot of insurance forms. Where's Mrs. Candlemass? The assistant manager."

"We sent her away. This is no place for civilians. Are you with the locals?"

"Yeah, I'm with 'em."

"Think there's really a bomb? There almost always isn't." He sounded young.

"This isn't one of the almosts."

He returned to his post behind the velvet ropes.

I dusted myself off and stood in the middle of the lobby, looking around the powder room of the Taj Mahal.

Something moved behind the candy counter; a shadow. I walked up to it and leaned my hands on the glass. Someone in an usher's uniform knelt in a fetal position on the floor, hands clasped behind his neck.

I tapped the glass with the barrel of the Chief's Special.

The figure stirred, unclasped its hands, and looked up at me. It was a college-age boy, breathing so shallowly he had hiccups. His face matched his buzz cut, which he'd bleached albino-white. His eyes were blue, the pupils shrunk with fear.

"Why haven't you evacuated?" I asked.

"I kind of did." He hiccuped. "Please don't kill me."

"Relax. I'm with the cops. How do I get up to the projection room?"

"There's just the one set of stairs, from the auditorium. Through the hidden door."

"What about backstage?"

He pointed to a door marked AUTHORIZED PERSONNEL ONLY.

"Thanks." I put away the revolver. "Got any Milk Duds?"

He hesitated, took a box off the stack inside the counter, and slid it onto the top. "That'll be three-sixty." He hiccuped.

The glamour of the place fell off abruptly when I went through the door. The passage, used exclusively by employees, took a backseat to the several millions the community had invested in restoring the building. Chewing the choc-olates to keep my mouth from drying out, I passed be-tween plasterboard walls, unpainted and patched, my way lit by pale fluorescents behind frosted glass panels in the ceiling. The floor was bare plywood. This part was un-heated and smelled and felt damp.

Shouts reverberated through uninsulated walls. They might have belonged to the feature soundtrack, but none was playing; at least none but in Jerry Marcus' head.

"Stay where you are! I'll shoot her in the head and throw her down the stairs like a sack of potatoes! Bumpity-bumpity-bump!" It was the first time I'd heard his voice. It cracked, as if it were changing. A toad crawled down my back and curled up at the base of my spine.

"Don't do it, Jerry! This doesn't have to be any worse than it is!" Lieutenant Karyl sounded calmer when he raised his voice than when he was speaking normally.

The passage ended at a steel fire door. It was locked, in the tradition of fire doors everywhere. I slipped the latch with the narrow strip of aluminum I keep in my wal-let. A theater smell puffed out when I opened the door, of dry-rot and old sweat and turpentine. Marcus' voice was louder now. I tuned out on the words; from here on they'd only get in the way.

There was more room than I expected behind the screen and the bare brick wall in back; I'd forgotten that the places were designed to provide every kind of public entertain-ment there was, with big band performances, dance num-bers, and acrobatic acts.

Nothing so gaudy was going on at the moment, or had

since Herbert Hoover. It was storage space now: a tangle of thick ropes like ship's rigging, canvas flats in stacks on the floor and leaning against the bricks, cartons filled with mildewing playbills, and an obstacle course of broken seats, piled lumber, and old stage properties left there to skin knees, bark ankles, and snag holes with exposed nail-heads. I tore a hole in my suitcoat clambering over it all to get to the corner, where a steel ladder bolted to the wall led straight up into darkness beyond catwalks arranged in a grid. Loops of insulated cable hung from these.

I took off the coat and my tie, let them drop, and started climbing.

The rungs were clammy and scabbed with rust. They wouldn't be used as frequently as when live shows meant changing backdrops and a stagehand to install ropes and pulleys; but they seemed sturdy enough. I stopped to peel a cobweb from across my eyes, and again to wipe my palms on my shirt. I reached back to make sure my revolver was snug in its clip and climbed higher.

Something scampered across my knuckles, following a ledge made by old mortar squirted out between courses of brick. I didn't look to see what it was. One phobia at a time was as much as I could handle.

A shot rang bells in my ears, close enough I took it at first for an explosion; Jerry Marcus' bomb going off. But then, I wouldn't hear it, would I? More reports answered, sounding farther away; a routine exchange. The ceiling— or unexposed rafters, more likely—was invisible up there where the lights didn't reach, but I must have been nearly level with the projection booth.

I don't like heights, never have; but I hung by one hand in order to turn my body to gauge just how far I was from Marcus' shooting stand.

Not so bad.

Just the entire length of the auditorium from front to back. I turned back toward the ladder and hauled myself up another rung.

The catwalks hung from ropes, all of which looked as new as the forty-hour work week. I made a long leg onto the one nearest the ladder, groping for one of the ropes supporting it. It swayed, creaking like an old schooner in rough seas. I held onto the rope with both hands until it stopped. I worked my way along the old boards, grasping the next rope before letting go of the last, feeling for spongy spots in the wood. A drop of sweat rolled off the end of my nose and shot fifteen feet down to the stage. It hit the boards with a plop that sounded as loud to me as any gun report. They knew how to build in acoustics then. The bastards.

I waited; but then Jerry Marcus started shouting again. He was getting louder by the yard; louder, I thought, than it should have been, coming from inside a room sealed in solid concrete. I took hope; but it might have been wishful thinking.

The catwalk took a turn at the end, butting onto another that ran parallel to the back of the auditorium where the projection room was. It was dark in the corner. I reached for a rope, missed it, gasped—and smacked my palm against brick. I was closer to the wall than I thought. From then on I groped my way along the wall.

My hand came up against something that stuck out from the brick. I wrapped my palm around it; the blunt end of something that turned out to be slim and cylindrical as I felt along it. When my hand touched cold steel I grasped the handle in both hands and lifted. Something came clear of the hooks or whatever had been holding it in place. I took down the fire axe and resumed progress, holding it horizontally across my waist. It made a dandy balancing rod.

More shots. I stopped until they did. I wondered how many reloads Marcus had with him. Plenty, probably. He seemed to have seen to everything else. Another lull, and then I crept on.

Something snapped with a bang I thought at first was another shot; but the catwalk took a sudden, stomach-lurching tilt. A rope had given way.

But the boards held. I rearranged my grip on the axe, sliding one hand up to the base of the blade and releasing the other to steady myself against the wall.

The surface changed abruptly: coarser, the spaces between the mortar more spread out. I had run out of brick and was supporting myself against the concrete blocks that enclosed the projection room. I stretched my arm farther along, testing the surface with my palm. It was unbroken. If I got to work with the axe right away, I might break through before Christmas.

Which Crystal the ticket clerk and I would never live to celebrate.

---

Marcus raised his voice again. This time I picked out the words.

"How do you like *this* show, Ann Arbor?" He fired a shot.

My chest seized up; I gripped the axe handle hard enough it's a wonder it didn't crack.

Then I heard a whimper and a tone of pleading. A woman's voice. It had been just another potshot, to punctuate what he'd said.

A low, shuddering whimper. A pleading tone. A woman's voice, weakening under the strain.

Heard.

Through concrete block.

I bent a knee, laying the axe across the boards at my feet. Groped again at the wall, widening my reach. Cold concrete. Porous; but not porous enough to let in oxygen to feed an out-of-control blaze or to let out a sound coming from anything less than the top of the lungs of a fanatic. Even the shot had seemed to come within inches of my ear.

I bent the other knee, lowering myself to the catwalk with my feet hanging over the edge. I took a deep breath, lifted my steadying hands from the boards, and pressed my palms against the wall. It was smoother than what I'd been feeling, and by comparison warm to the touch. I tapped it with a finger. A hollow noise.

Measuring now. I spread my palms out from the center, up and down, feeling for the seam where the block left off and plaster began. It was plaster for sure. Somewhere, in the act of remodeling, someone had broken through, probably to make room for an escape hatch for the projectionist if a fire had broken out, then plastered it over to prevent unwanted access from my side. Something had scampered across the top of my hand when I was climbing the ladder. Nobody likes sharing his workplace with rats.

No one likes the idea of burning to death, either; but someone had dropped the ball, neglecting to go through with the safety plan. Mrs. Candlemass would want to know about this. There were insurance issues involved, and legal complications.

I climbed back to my feet, bringing with me the axe; a shakier operation than the reverse. It put extra pressure on the remaining ropes holding up the catwalk. Upright at last, I spread my feet, took a deep breath, and swung the axe.

# TWENTY-EIGHT

**W**hat do you want, Jerry?"

A calm voice but a powerful one: I felt it in the soles of my feet. Lieutenant Karyl had scored a bullhorn.

I stopped the axe in midswing; a disc shifted in my spine. I grasped a rope while the pain diffused itself through all my extremities.

"I want—"

Marcus reeled off a list of names, most of which meant nothing to me. I recognized the mayor's. It might as well have been the president's. He'd made up his mind. He was just enjoying the moment of power before digging Crater Lake into the middle of the city. Next he would call for the pope. It could be one of the dead ones for all it mattered.

"What do you want them for, Jerry?"

"Tell them they're invited to a world premiere!"

*"Please!"*

Crystal's voice, stretched thin.

Something thumped; the butt of a revolver? A whimper stopped in the middle.

"I didn't get all those names, Jerry," Karyl said. "Can you repeat?" He sounded as calm as a lagoon at midnight.

"I don't chew my cabbage twice! If any of them—any one!—doesn't show, I'll put a hole in Little Miss Box Office's head. How do you think that'll go over with the critics?"

"Gratuitous violence, Jerry. You know the language."

A shot destroyed some more historical architecture.

"Stop dicking around! You know my demands!"

"It'll take time to reach them all. We don't want to go to all the trouble if you get impatient and do something you can't undo."

Marcus laughed; high and shrill. I felt again something scampering across my hand. Whether he was as mad as Mab or acting, it all amounted to the same thing. I set down the axe, propping it between my knees, mopped my palms on my thighs, and picked it back up.

"Been there, done that," he said. "Ask Tom. Ask Moze."

"If you're confessing to the murders of your brother and Alec Moselle, we can still work something out. Jerry, you're not capable of making a rational decision. We've got people who can help you through that. You're not a criminal, just someone who needs help."

"I'm just fine. It's the rest of the world needs help. Are you going to give me what I want or not? This vest is getting hot."

"So take it off. Who's stopping you?"

"Enough. The show always starts on time."

I cocked the axe behind my hip; fisted it in both hands.

"How about letting the young lady go while we're waiting?"

A bullet pierced the plaster patch two inches shy of my left knee. I froze with the axe cocked.

It was a wild shot. He was so far gone he'd slung it away from the projector opening, toward what should have been concrete block. By all rights the slug should have spanged around the booth, endangering captive and captor.

Silence followed.

I lowered the axe; drew the revolver.

Crazy isn't stupid. He'd investigate.

Something made a scratching sound. It might have been a rat gnawing at one of the ropes that held me up.

I hoped that's all it was.

I scrambled aside of the patch of plaster an instant before a hole tore through it. I heard the shot, and the slug burying itself in the wall backstage.

In the dim light, something stuck itself through the bullet hole; a finger, probing into nothingness.

He didn't know I was there. I had that on my side, also the distraction from the auditorium and his captive. I breathed as shallowly as possible.

Waiting. With an axe in one hand and a revolver in the other.

A moment of silence, followed by an explosion.

I flinched; who wouldn't, knowing what the well-dressed homicidal maniac was wearing that season? A foot in a thick-soled combat boot poked through a hole in the plaster, spilling out a ragged oval of light from the other side. He had a powerful kick, but fast reflexes also; the foot withdrew before I could swing the axe.

Something heavy scraped the floor on the other side of the partition, eclipsing the light from inside. He was fortifying that position.

I dropped the axe, holstered the revolver, grasped two ropes, swung back, swung forward, back again, and Errol-Flynned my way, feet foremost, through the plaster.

I stuck the landing, standing in the middle of a concrete pillbox staring at Jerry Marcus: his mouth open, face distended, one hand holding his full-bellied Magnum, the other the remote, programmed to the ordnance on his vest. A rolling metal rack lay on its side in a litter of film cans. I'd knocked it over before he could finish blocking the entrance.

The room was tiny, just big enough for the man in charge to turn from the projector to the film rack. The projector itself, a monster Bell & Howell the size of a VW Beetle, took up most of the space, shining its steel-beam-solid shaft of light through a small aperture in the concrete wall onto the screen on the other side of the auditorium; the heat of its bulb turned the room into an oven. Jerry Marcus had sweat clear through his explosive vest, a khaki one with lots of pockets like photographers wore to carry their extra lenses, cameras, and rolls of film; he'd probably taken it from Moze's studio along with the chemicals he'd needed. A tangle of wires stretched from a flap pocket on his chest to both bulging side pockets.

His hostage, a thin blond young woman in a loose flannel shirt and ripped jeans, was drenched also. Her eyes stared from their sockets in a face distended with terror.

"Drop it!" Jerry gripped both weapons tight.

I had the .38 half out. I drew it the rest of the way between two fingers and let it fall. His eyes followed the movement. In that instant I shoved the massive projector around on its swivel.

A quarter-ton of Hollywood technology swung his way. He ducked it, but he stumbled against the concrete wall, dropping the remote and the revolver.

I lunged to catch the remote before it hit the floor.

I missed; but the only noise it made when it struck was a rattle. I lunged for it.

I was closer, but Marcus' reflexes held up. He kicked it into a corner. I raced him. This time he was closer. He came up with it as my hand whiffed past him.

There was only one button, a yellow one the size of a dime. His thumb pressed down on it.

Nothing happened.

He pressed it again and again, shaking the remote. Then he looked down at his vest. The wires were gone. He looked at me.

I opened my hand and let them fall to the floor.

He snatched up the Magnum while I was still reaching for my .38. The gun roared, echoing off concrete.

In the instant, I almost groped at my chest for the bullet.

My ears rang. I looked down at Jerry Marcus, sprawled on the pile of film reels with a blue-black hole in the center of his forehead.

Later, the cleanup team found three nicks in the concrete walls where his slug had ricocheted before it spent itself, a misshapen lump of lead and copper lying like a dead bee on the floor. It had missed the girl and me by inches. He was already dead when his finger pressed the trigger.

I'd forgotten about the big projector. When I'd spun it away from the square opening to the auditorium, the bright shaft had gone with it. I turned around and looked into the face of a man in an ERT uniform in the balcony on the other side. His scoped rifle rested on the railing, aimed for a second shot. I raised my hands.

# TWENTY-NINE

et's go, Crystal. We're in the way."

The young woman had backed herself into a corner, hugging her knees. Her eyes moved slowly toward the dead man on the floor, but I was standing in front of him. The sniper was wired for sound; he'd lowered his rifle and given me the wave.

After a long time the ticket clerk stirred. Her hand was clammy. I pulled her to her feet, still blocking her view of Marcus, and we went down by way of the stairs leading to the auditorium, she leaning on me with most of her weight.

"How did you know my name?" Her voice was little-girl small. I had to strain to hear it.

"Oh, you're famous."

Halfway down I stopped and pulled her with me against the wall. The stairwell had gotten crowded suddenly.

The Detroit Bomb Squad came up, hut-hutting military fashion in their *RoboCop* outfits, carrying shields and a stainless-steel container the size of a trash basket.

An Ann Arbor uniform shooed us out of the building. There a female officer relieved me of Crystal. Lately I couldn't seem to hang onto a woman more than a few minutes.

It looked as if the city had been occupied by a foreign power. There wasn't a civilian in sight. They'd been cleared from the area for four blocks all around. Bullhorns squealed feedback, distorting warnings to keep things that way.

Or maybe they weren't distorted at all. I kept wondering who was playing the cymbals until I realized they were crashing for me alone, a command performance.

After twenty minutes the bomb squad came out, two men walking abreast inside a protective circle, each with both hands on a handle of the container. They bucket-brigaded it up to a man standing in the top hatch of the armored carrier. Just another day on the job, which turned over every couple of weeks. The local uniforms applauded as the big ugly half-track rolled away.

I was still there, smoking my tenth cigarette in a half hour, when they brought the body down in a zipper bag on an aluminum stretcher. They loaded it into a boxy county ambulance and slammed the doors shut on Jerry Marcus.

# THIRTY

Can you say it again? I still can't hear anything on that side."

Lieutenant Karyl raised his voice. "I said we found out where Marcus was holed up: House in Saline, a mortgage-foreclosure job, been on the market three months. He broke in through a back door. He left behind a coffee can with better than sixty grand in it in cash; had to have been him, otherwise the payments would have been made. Next order of business is tracking down all his suckers and making a fair distribution."

We were in his office in the municipal building. It had been three days and the blinding flash of an explosion was still jerking me out of a sound sleep.

"Whatever you do," I said, "some of them won't think it's fair."

"Who gives a shit?" He waved a hand at yesterday's *Ann Arbor News* and *Detroit Free Press* on his desk. "Both the local editor and this guy Stackpole quote an anonymous source using almost the same words. You're pretty good at spreading the wealth yourself."

"I had promises to keep."

"And miles to go before you sleep."

I put out my cigarette in a glass tray with a block M in the base. "I keep forgetting they teach cops to read here."

"The Crystal girl's going to be all right. Her parents picked her up from St. Joe, where they had her under observation overnight. They're sorting through invitations for her to appear on *Today* and *Good Morning America*."

"Kids. They bounce back."

"Speaking of which, we know now why Marcus laid off the Zacharias girl. She stopped mattering when he decided to take himself out with the building. He had the detonator hooked up to an ordinary nine-volt battery, that's all he needed. The Detroit bomb guys blew up his vest on state land outside Chelsea. That's about thirty miles from here. People heard it here in town."

The young cop who had asked me about moonlighting came in with my statement typed out. I read it, signed it, and handed back the lieutenant's pen. He slid the stapled sheets into a cardboard folder. "Well, that's that." He gave me his Gypsy stare.

"Yeah, yeah." I got up. "Save the sundown speech. I'm headed home."

"I was going to say, 'Come back for Octoberfest.' I'll buy you a beer. That was a fool play you made, but it saved everybody trouble. What made you go for the wires instead of the remote?"

"I didn't. First I knew I had 'em was when I looked down and saw them in my hand."


Jerry Marcus' mother made arrangements to have him and his twin brother sent back to North Dakota for burial.

One of Alec Moselle's admirers, a University of Michigan alumnus with too much money for his tax bracket, donated a million dollars to establish a photography scholarship in his name. Several applicants submitted shots taken of naked people in shopping malls and on freeway entrance ramps, thinking that would please Moze's restless spirit, but the board in charge of the scholarship gave the spot to a young woman who specialized in landscapes. By then, *Ann Arbor Exposed,* the dead man's collection of candid nudes, was in stores, and I suppose they didn't want to take the chance of reviving the tradition of the Naked Mile.

I never heard from Dante and Heloise Gunnar again, even though they got back most of the fifteen thousand they'd dropped on Marcus' movie. I did get a call from Hernando Suiz, their attorney, kicking about some items on the expense sheet. I ate the Ypsilanti motel bill, but got him to reimburse me for Holly Zacharias' train fare to Chicago. I struck him off as a future reference.

All this happened a long time ago.

Borders is gone, Thano's Lamplighter, too. They tore all the swanky public telephone booths out of the Michigan Union and just about everywhere else, forcing me to join the cellular revolution.

After 149 years, the *Ann Arbor News* shut down, to reappear later as a dot-com publication, printing two editions per week. Aunt Agatha's mystery bookshop is still there, but I haven't been back to it. I didn't take Karyl up on that beer offer either.

The Michigan Theater still stands, a monument to the days when going to the movies was a dress-up affair, and the destination rewarded the effort; the coalition that owns it has even added a second screen since I visited, along with a proper escape hatch in the projection booth. One of Jerry Marcus' pigeons donated part of his reimbursement toward repairing the damage to the auditorium caused by gunfire; the artisan who restored the architectural details was the great-grandson of one of the original workmen from 1928.

The standoff on Liberty Street was reported widely. Inspired by the publicity, a West Coast production company bought the rights to *Mr. Alien Elect* from Marcus' mother and announced plans to finish it, using area locations to take advantage of Michigan's generous Hollywood stimulus plan to boost its economy; but then the administration changed in Lansing and the plan was struck down. The company wrote off the project.

Holly Zacharias sent me an invitation to her graduation ceremony. I thought of attending, but that day I was in Columbus, Ohio, tracing a series of safe-deposit boxes belonging to a Detroit city councilman who'd let his house on Bagley go into foreclosure. I sent Holly a funny card, but she didn't write back.

I've been back to Ann Arbor only once, chasing a bad lead on a missing-person case. As long as I was there I called the police department, hoping to make up for that

Octoberfest no-show, but I was told Lieutenant Karyl had left to accept a position as police chief in a small town in Wisconsin. Zingerman's is still where I left it; I ate a barbecue sandwich and drove back to Detroit.

Last week a thick envelope came to the office with a DVD inside in a plastic case. It turned out to be a week's worth of five-minute stock market reports delivered by a young woman at a TV station in Evanston, Illinois. Holly had let her hair grow out and replaced the studs in her face with a light application of makeup. There was no note, but she put in a picture postcard from SeaWorld. It had been just long enough I had almost forgotten the point of the joke.

# AUTHOR'S NOTE

The Sundown Speech is a greatly expanded reimagi-
nation of *Attitude*, a novella I wrote on commission
for the old *Ann Arbor News* in 2004. It ran in install-
ments throughout twenty editions of the newspaper, with
members of the staff and their families appearing in pho-
tos representing the characters. It was my first experience
with that centuries-old publishing tradition, serial fiction,
and I enjoyed the experience very much.

Although I haven't confirmed it personally, I'm quite
sure that all precautions have been taken from the start to
ensure the safety of projectionists and all others employed
by the Michigan Theater. I apologize if my use of literary
license in order to ramp up suspense has offended anyone.

I'd like to thank Judy McGovern, that "pleasant-faced
woman with the eyes of a peregrine falcon," who oversaw
the serial project in her position as features editor, all the
*News* employees and their families who took part, and
those good sports who wrote to the newspaper to express

their forgiveness for the gentle fun I poked at the "Ann Arbor attitude."

I'm a third-generation Arborite: I was born there in 1952, my father in 1910, and his father in 1867. The city may not be the cultural center of the world, but it has a rich culture, as well as a warm heart.

No aliens were harmed in the telling of his story.